T0120451

ALL THE
DEAD
SHALL
WEEP

ALSO BY CHARLAINE HARRIS

Gunnie Rose series

An Easy Death
A Longer Fall
The Russian Cage
The Serpent in Heaven

A Novel of Midnight, Texas series

Midnight Crossroad
Day Shift
Night Shift

A Sookie Stackhouse Novel series

Dead until Dark
Living Dead in Dallas
Club Dead
Dead to the World
Dead as a Doornail
Definitely Dead
All Together Dead
From Dead to Worse

Dead and Gone
Dead in the Family
Dead Reckoning
Deadlocked
Dead Ever After
The Complete Sookie Stackhouse Stories
The Sookie Stackhouse Companion

An Aurora Teagarden Mystery series

Real Murders
A Bone to Pick
Three Bedrooms, One Corpse
The Julius House
Dead over Heels
A Fool and His Honey
Last Scene Alive
Poppy Done to Death
All the Little Liars
Sleep Like a Baby

Gunnie Rose:

BOOK 5

ALL THE DEAD SHALL WEEP

CHARLAINE
HARRIS

SAGA PRESS

LONDON SYDNEY **NEW YORK** TORONTO NEW DELHI

SAGA PRESS
AN IMPRINT OF SIMON & SCHUSTER, LLC

1230 AVENUE OF THE AMERICAS, NEW YORK, NEW YORK 10020

This book is a work of fiction. Any references to historical events, real people, or real places are used fictitiously. Other names, characters, places, and events are products of the author's imagination, and any resemblance to actual events or places or persons, living or dead, is entirely coincidental.

First Saga Press trade paperback edition July 2024

SAGA PRESS and colophon are trademarks of Simon & Schuster, LLC

Simon & Schuster: Celebrating 100 Years of Publishing in 2024

For information about special discounts for bulk purchases, please contact Simon & Schuster Special Sales at 1-866-506-1949 or business@simonandschuster.com.

The Simon & Schuster Speakers Bureau can bring authors to your live event. For more information or to book an event, contact the Simon & Schuster Speakers Bureau at 1-866-248-3049 or visit our website at www.simonspeakers.com.

Interior design by Yvonne Taylor

Manufactured in the United States of America

1   3   5   7   9   10   8   6   4   2

Library of Congress Cataloging-in-Publication Data is available.

ISBN 978-1-9821-8252-6
ISBN 978-1-9821-8253-3 (pbk)
ISBN 978-1-9821-8254-0 (ebook)

To Paula, who travels with me and hears me groan and moan. To Toni and Dana, who offer me the best of constructive criticism and invaluable friendship. To my husband and children and grandchildren, who hold my heart. To my agent, Joshua Bilmes of JABberwocky, who has been my strong right hand during my whole career. To Debbie and Steve at APA, for their diligence on my behalf. And last and foremost, to my readers, without whom I am nothing.

ALL THE DEAD SHALL WEEP

CHAPTER ONE

Lizbeth

Eli was working, so I met the train at Sweetwater by myself. I'd just returned from guarding a shipment of farm implements on a leg of its journey between Canada and Mexico; I'd had to travel to take the job, but it had been ten days of work, and lucrative. And it had gotten me out of the house.

All of which meant I could afford to rent the old car from the Segundo Mexia stables and drive to Sweetwater to meet the train.

The station at Sweetwater was little more than a shack clinging to a platform, but at least there were a couple of benches under a roof. I was grateful for the shade. It was June, and June in Texoma is hot and dry . . . unless it rains. Then it's hot and steamy. Today was a dry day.

The stationmaster, a sprightly sixty-ish woman named Molly Lerma, came out of the shack to sit with me. I expect she was glad of the company.

"You're Jackson and Candle's daughter, ain't you?" she asked, and spat into an old can positioned at her feet.

"Candle's daughter and Jackson's stepdaughter. Lizbeth Rose. Lizbeth Rose Savarova, now." My outlandish married name still got a lot of stares in Texoma, which used to be Texas and Oklahoma, more or less.

Molly Lerma gave me the expected long stare. "You the one married that wizard?"

I wasn't going to tell her that Eli was a grigori, not a wizard, especially since I wasn't sure there was a big difference. "Eli Savarov," I said. I didn't tack the "Prince" on first because it just sounded silly.

"And he wanted to live in Texoma?"

I wasn't surprised Molly sounded incredulous. Texoma was poor, remote, and the smallest of the five countries created when the United States had fallen apart.

"He did," I said, and left it at that.

"How's Jackson doing? I knew him from school," the stationmaster said. She spat again.

"He's doing well." Jackson had worked hard and carved himself out a position of power in Segundo Mexia, our little town.

Molly smiled. She was missing some important teeth. "Jackson always was a go-getter."

I nodded and smiled back, hoping the conversation was at an end. Not that I minded talking about my stepfather. I was real fond of Jackson Skidder. He'd taught me how to shoot and given me my Colts. Couldn't ask for anything better than my Colt 1911s. I had to stop myself from reaching down to pat them. Jackson had been way more of a dad to me than my actual father, whom I'd only met once, the day I killed him.

After a pleasant few minutes of silence, I asked Molly if the train was on time. She said, "I reckon." That was the end of our conversation. Which suited me. I had a lot to think about.

I was waiting at the train station to pick up my half sister Felicia, who was coming in from San Diego (capital of the Holy Russian Empire) with Eli's brother Peter. Not only had Eli and I not had company since we'd been married, but Felicia was over fifteen, and Peter was eighteen and a bit. The last time I'd seen them, they'd been sweet on each other. Their sleeping arrangements were kind of up in the air.

Also, though my half sister (same father, different mother) had started life in a Mexican slum, she was an educated city girl now. Segundo Mexia, my hometown, was humble and small, as Eli had carefully not said during the past few months. After we'd come home married and built the addition to my cabin and Eli had begun scouting around for work, I'd seen lots of mouth-tightening and tense shoulders. He was having a hard time adjusting.

During their stay, would Peter and Felicia be content to hunt with me or practice magic with Eli? Did you have to entertain company?

I knew that moving dirt, finding water, and warding businesses was not what Eli, now Prince Savarov, had planned to do as a grigori. In his life in San Diego, Eli had been in Tsar Alexei's service. He'd had access to the palace and a relationship with the royal family. He'd had good friends among the other grigoris, the top of the magic hierarchy. He'd had a disagreeable but powerful partner named Paulina. He'd been able to visit his mother and sisters and Peter. He'd lived in the grigori dormitory. He'd been independent and important and on the way up.

Now Eli lived in Segundo Mexia with me, doing work that was anything but exalted. The people in my little town were just getting over regarding Eli with suspicion. Grigoris were not highly regarded in Texoma, unlike in the Holy Russian Empire. Of course, Eli lived with me, his wife, and I had only a trace of magic. I was a gunnie. I made my living—our living—with my shooting. In Texoma, that had more prestige.

Eli hadn't complained about any of this. It was the silence that worried me.

If I ran out of concerns about my husband, I could fret about how my mother would feel when she met Felicia, the other daughter of my father. I'd been conceived when Oleg Karkarov raped my mother. Later, back in Mexico, Oleg had married Felicia's mother before Felicia had come along. My mother had been beautiful; Felicia's mother had been the scion of Mexico's most prominent witch family.

I could see a black dot way down the tracks. I breathed out, relieved and worried and happy.

"Thar she comes," Molly Lerma said. "Right on time." She sounded triumphant, as if I'd told her I doubted the train would arrive.

"Right on time," I agreed.

Hooting and screeching, the train came to a stop at the little station. Old Mrs. Guthrie got off first. Molly Lerma helped her down the steps. Mrs. Guthrie carried an ancient carpetbag and a cage with a bird in it. You would have thought she was carrying a horse, the fuss she made.

I was on my feet and waiting impatiently for her to clear the way, because I knew my sister would be next off. Felicia propelled herself from the steps, and I caught her, and we laughed and held each other, and she cried a little before she drew back. Felicia was so grown-up! So pretty! We didn't look alike . . . but we did, in some ways.

By that time, Peter had gotten off, too. He was carrying two modest suitcases. He gave me a quick hug and a peck on the cheek before looking up and down the little platform. "Where's Eli?" he said.

"Oh, my God!" Felicia was bouncing up and down on the balls of her feet. There was more of her to bounce than there had been a few months ago, especially in the chest department. "We're here! We're out of the city!"

That made me feel a little better. "I'm really glad to see you," I said. "Peter, Eli's working, but he'll be home soon. Maybe by the time we get there."

Peter smiled. That turned him into a man you'd look at a second time.

My half sister sure looked . . . and smiled back.

"This all your luggage?" I pointed at the two bags Peter carried.

"Peter said I had to travel light." Felicia was still bouncing.

I asked Peter to put the bags in the car, and after some exclaiming over the luxury of getting to ride—which was a real luxury in Texoma, they both realized—Peter tossed the bags into the trunk, and we admired the car, which had been created out of bits and pieces of vehicles that had gone before. The body had come from a Ford, but the doors had been grafted on from another car line, and so on.

"Let's get going," I said. I opened the driver's door. Peter went around to the other side.

"Who is your doctor?" Peter asked as he slid into the front seat.

"What doctor?" I sounded angry, and I knew it. I couldn't help it. I was going to have to talk about what had happened.

They both froze. They glanced at each other. Then back at me.

Felicia said, very slowly, very cautiously, "Lizbeth, it seems to Peter and me that you are pregnant."

"I'm not," I said, and then I fainted.

It only took me a minute to come around, and then I scrambled to my feet, weaving as I stood, just for a moment. Felicia was kneeling beside the open car door, Peter looked horrified, and stationmaster Molly was gaping.

"Liar," Felicia said, standing to put her arm around me. In a vague sort of way, I noticed she didn't have to reach up to do that now. She was six years younger than me, but she was going to pass me height-wise, probably in the next few months.

That was not what I was supposed to be thinking about.

"I'm really not," I said.

"But you fainted."

"I lost the baby fifteen days ago," I said, in a voice that told them to close the subject. I got back in the driver's seat.

"Do you think I ought to drive?" Peter offered. "I'd be glad to do that."

"I feel fine now." And I did. Almost normal. I looked in the rearview mirror at my sister, who was trying not to cry.

After a moment's hesitation, Peter climbed in beside me. The car started up just fine. The soft upholstery smelled like dust, probably because the windows had to be left open for air circulation. We drove out of Sweetwater with my two visitors looking around them at the gently rolling countryside, the patches of green (mostly mountain cedar), the dry grass, the beating sun.

"How's Eli?" Peter said. "Where is he working?" He yawned widely.

"He had to go over to Cactus Flats early this morning. He's doing some earthmoving to help with their new town sewage system."

"An air grigori working on earth?" Peter frowned.

"It's a job that pays," I said, as mildly as I could. Though Eli's specialty was air, that didn't mean he couldn't move some earth. Just required a little more work. Same way I'd taken on a job guarding a bank in Homer's Corner while there was a large payroll in its safe, which was not my favorite job. It was what I called a sitting duck situation.

But Eli and I needed extra money to pay for the expense of additions to our cabin. Until the year before, my home had been one large room with a walled-off bathroom in one corner. In time, I'd gotten on city water.

Even later, after I'd met Eli and he'd come to care about me (and I'd done him some favors), he'd added electricity. Several of the houses on the hill had tied into it, too. So my monthly bills, which had been almost nonexistent, were now a factor in my budget. But I hunted for my meat, I'd gotten some vegetables in return for helping with my mother's garden, and I swapped for other things I needed.

That had been good living for a single woman but not ideal for a couple, we'd found. It had been easy enough to add our bedroom, but it had put a hole in our savings. Now we'd added yet another bedroom to the cabin. We were managing, but we had to consider every expenditure. Eli wasn't used to that.

I realized neither Peter nor Felicia had spoken in a few minutes. Felicia's eyes were shut, and she'd leaned against the door. Peter's eyes were open but droopy.

"You tired?" I asked him.

He nodded. In another minute, his eyes closed. I remembered how exhausted I'd been when I'd traveled to San Diego and back.

Felicia stirred a little when we got to the outskirts of Segundo Mexia. "We there?" she said, her voice full of sleep.

"Yep. You and Peter share a bed?" I asked Felicia quietly. I wanted to get that settled before we got home. "We can put a partition between two beds in the new room, or we can shove the beds together. We didn't want to take anything for granted."

Felicia was nodding off again. "We can share," she muttered. "Either way is fine. When will we meet your mother?"

"Tomorrow," I said. "When you've woken up."

"'Kay," she said, and her eyes shut.

The rest of the ride was completely silent. It was brief, too, because there wasn't much to Segundo Mexia even when you drove through the whole town, as I had. I hated to wake my passengers, but we'd have to walk up to the cabin. There was no track for a car. None of us who lived up the hill had one. Not enough money.

I roused my passengers to start them walking. I followed with the bags. We passed Rex Santino on his way to town and exchanged greetings. Jed Franklin was working on some leather at a table outside his cabin, and we nodded at each other. Chrissie popped out of her front (and only) door long enough to wave at me, shake her head at the sight of my guests (who were just about walking in their sleep), and begin to hang out her wash. Her two boys were at school, though it was about to close for the summer.

My mother, the town schoolteacher, had told me Chrissie's boys were not too bright, very lively, and good-natured. Took after their ma, in other words. Chrissie's youngest, a girl, began to cry from inside the shack. Chrissie pegged one last shirt on the line and went in.

Our cabin was the last one on the town side of the hill, near the top. I was glad to see the front door open as we approached. Eli leaped out to hug Peter, then Felicia.

"They need to go right to bed," I called.

"I can see that." Eli was smiling. He was *very* happy to see his brother. He'd talked about his sisters and his mother from time to time, but I think he'd missed Peter most of all. Eli raised his eyebrows over Peter's head, silently asking if I'd gotten the word on the bed situation. I held up a finger for one. He nodded and made big eyes at me to show his astonishment.

I laughed out loud. I couldn't help it. I was so glad to see Eli acting like himself.

Felicia turned to look, her eyes heavy with sleep. "Bathroom?" she said groggily.

"Indoors to the back right," I said. It made me proud to need to give directions to the inside of the cabin. Before, it had been completely obvious where everything must be. Having a bathroom inside was not a given in Segundo Mexia or anywhere in Texoma.

Eli was showing Peter their bedroom (to the right of the big original room). He stowed the suitcases on the bench at the foot of the bed, which we had built . . . both bed and bench. Without another word, Peter collapsed onto the mattress. At least he'd pulled his shoes off.

After a couple of minutes, Felicia trudged out of the bathroom and into the bedroom, her face clean. When she saw Peter asleep, she half-smiled before she slid into the bed beside him. Eli and I backed out and shut the door behind us.

That was the last we saw of our company until early evening.

Eli and I ate sandwiches outside at the picnic table under the live oak tree. He'd gotten cash for the job this morning, which was not always the case. Sometimes he was paid in produce or chickens or rabbits. Once a goat. At first, this had astonished and disgusted him, but now he'd adapted. I'd dug a pit and barbecued the goat, and it had been delicious. We'd fed everyone on the hill. Jackson and my mother had come, too.

"What shall I do?" Eli said after we'd eaten. He glanced at the house, hopeful he'd see Peter come out. He would be restless until he could talk to his brother. This was a thing I'd learned about Eli after we'd gotten married: he was not good at just being. He didn't mind a good project, but he was not one to just take a morning off to fish or hunt.

"You can return the car to John Seahorse," I said. "Tell him it drove fine. And if you could drop by the hotel to tell Jackson our company got here safely, I'd appreciate it." I handed him the car key.

Eli jumped up and started downhill. There was a breeze, and his long light hair blew back in a pretty way. He was wearing his grigori vest, of course, with its many pockets and crannies, over a sleeveless shirt. He was a sight. I sighed at the picture he made.

Jackson and my mom seemed to like him, though there was a certain reservation in the way they treated him. I sighed again, this time not so happily.

I went into the cabin to wash our plates and found that Felicia had tossed their travel clothes outside the bedroom door. I gathered them and heated water over the outside fire. I used it to fill the wash-tub outside, added some soap flakes, and plunged the clothes into the hot water. I scrubbed them and rinsed them and hung them to dry, which wouldn't take any time at all on this hot, sunny day.

I thought about the hundreds of times I'd watched my mother do the same thing. I didn't think Candle Rose Skidder (her name for fifteen years now) was exactly looking forward to meeting my half sister—yet she was glad that I had one, she'd told me so.

I was very lucky. Though I'd been the result of rape, I'd been brought up with love. My mother had trained to be a teacher so she could support me, and my grandparents had taken care of me while she did so. Mom might have hidden her head in disgrace all her days, but she did not. She toughed it out. She'd ended up respected, and she'd made a good marriage to Jackson Skidder.

My half sister, who was legitimate, had lost her mother and been neglected by our father. Her mother's father had denied her. I, the bastard, had come out the luckier of us two. I could only be grateful.

I yawned wide enough to swallow a deer whole. Maybe a nap would be a good idea. I lay down on our bed, leaving the door open. In two shakes of a lamb's tail, I was dreaming of broad deserts.

CHAPTER TWO

Though I had been asleep for an hour, Eli hadn't returned when I was wakened by a knock at the door. I pulled myself out of my doze to answer it as quickly as I could, so Felicia and Peter wouldn't be disturbed.

If I'd known the knocker was Thomas Carter, I wouldn't have opened the door. I regretted not having taken the time to buckle on my gun belt.

Thomas was the brother of one of my first bosses. I'd liked Martin Carter, both as a friend and a boss, but Thomas had always reminded me of a snake. He hadn't liked me when I worked for Martin. He liked me even less after Martin died and I inherited the proceeds of our last job and Martin's guns.

Then Thomas tried to best me by taking me to his bed. He had this delusion that he was attractive to me. He turned out to be one of those men who can't accept it when you aren't interested.

Today Thomas was smiling at me . . . that sneering kind of smile that made me want to slap the tar out of him. He knew he was about to ruin my day.

So I didn't speak.

After a moment or two, Thomas couldn't wait any longer. He wanted to drop whatever bomb he thought he had in his armory. "I hear you got company," he said.

I waited some more.

"Where's your Russian?" was Thomas's next clever remark.

So he knew Eli was gone. Maybe he'd seen Eli in town. "Home any minute," I said. I hoped I could make him leave. If I didn't lose my temper, Eli might.

"I'm just trying to be nice."

"You've never tried to be nice in your life."

"I hear you added a room on your house. Got a baby on the way?" He waggled his eyebrows.

He couldn't know he'd hit me in the stomach. I kept my face blank, but it cost me a lot.

"No baby. A brother-in-law visiting," Peter said from behind me.

"And who are you?" Thomas said.

"My brother-in-law, dumbass," I said, just as Peter answered, "What the fuck is it to you?"

I was surprised by the language, but I couldn't have put it better myself.

"I just come to tell you I'm running for sheriff, and I got some money behind me," Thomas said. "I hope I can count on your vote." He was still grinning.

I stared at him, willing him to keel over with a heart attack. When Thomas just kept smirking, I shut the door in his face. And leaned against it.

"I heard that right?" Peter said, as we listened to Thomas's footsteps retreating. "He's running for sheriff?"

"Yes. Maybe that's supposed to strike fear in my heart. The bad thing is, it does. He could find a hundred ways to make my life miserable if he gets elected."

We sat at the table in the middle of the room. I'd borrowed a checked tablecloth from my mother for the occasion, and I thought it dressed up the room—which, to be honest, was very plain.

"Jonah Gleason died last month. He'd been the sheriff here my whole life. Not that he had a lot to do. He pretty much let things roll along. But Jonah and I got along. Having a sheriff who flat-out hates me . . . that would be bad."

It was a good time for Eli to return.

"I passed Thomas Carter," my husband said. "He came here? He gave me a big smile. I guess he wanted to make sure I was worried about his visit." Eli bent to give his brother a hug. They beamed at each other.

"He came to threaten your wife," Peter said.

"Threaten Lizbeth? What a chump." Eli had a slight Russian accent. I pressed my lips together so I wouldn't smile.

"Thomas is running for sheriff," I explained.

The door to the guest bedroom opened. "Why?" Felicia said. Though she was rumpled and had pillow creases on her face, it struck me that my little sister was now quite pretty. I'd never thought about it before.

"Why what?" Eli said, leaning over to give her a hug and a kiss on the cheek.

"Why is this Thomas running for the office, you think?" Felicia had a brush in her hand, and now she began running it through her long, dark mane. I could see hairs drifting down to the floor in the sunlight. I suppressed a sigh.

"Thomas would love to have power," I said, not caring that I sounded sour. "He's never found anything he's good at, except being an ass. There's history behind him hating me. My first serious boyfriend was Tarken, who hired me onto his gun crew when I was sixteen. The other crew leader was Martin, Thomas's brother."

This was old information to Eli, who began putting away the clean pans still in the drainboard.

"How old was Tarken?" Felicia asked, in a very casual tone.

"Probably twenty-eight? Thereabouts, anyway."

Felicia tried to hide her disapproval. I let her.

"After I'd been on the crew awhile, Tarken and I got close. Then he was killed in an ambush on a run to New America. The rest of the crew—Martin and my friend Galilee—died, too. Everyone but me."

Eli opened the door to our bedroom to hang his hat and vest inside and returned to pat me on the shoulder. He knew this was painful for me still. He had met me soon after that awful time, when I'd still been suffering from the aftereffects.

"Were you hurt?" Peter said.

"I wasn't shot dead, like my friends. But I got a pretty bad knock on the head. I had to finish the job, which was getting two farm families to Corbin in New America. We ran into more trouble on the way." I hadn't thought we'd ever get to Corbin to meet up with Joshua Beekins, who'd hired our gun team.

"So how did Thomas come to be angry? Did he blame you for his brother's death?" Peter was sure that must be the reason Thomas hated me.

I shook my head. "Even for Thomas, that wouldn't make any sense. If you're a gunnie, you got to expect you're going to encounter close calls and death, as a matter of course." That was the nature of the job.

"Then *what*?" Felicia was impatient.

"Thomas buried Tarken and Martin, which ordinarily I would have done. But I had to hurry after our cargo, try to save them from the gang that attacked us. Thomas expected me to be very grateful that he'd dug the graves."

They stared at me.

"He expected me to show my gratitude with sex."

"Ewwwww," Felicia said.

"Instead, my stepfather sent Thomas a barrel of pickles."

Peter laughed. "A barrel of pickles instead of you!" He traded a smile with Eli, who'd always thought that part of the story was funny, too.

I nodded. "So I thought that was over. And I repaid Jackson for the pickles, killed him a deer and a turkey. I hoped I'd heard the last of Thomas until one night, he came by here drunk and told me I owed him Martin's gun. The gun was mine by right. The gun goes to the gun crew when a member dies."

I got up to start chopping the cooked beef roast I'd pulled out of the refrigerator. If it had been cold weather, I'd have been glad to put it in a pan in the oven, but when the temperature was this warm, cooking outside on the fire was better. I added some water and chopped onions and tomatoes and a pepper, then salt, cumin, and cilantro. Peter carried the pot out and put it where Eli showed him, above the fire Eli started with a spell. Nice to have extra hands.

"I did give one of the bandit pistols to Galilee's son," I told Felicia, in the interest of honesty. "And I gave Tarken's share of the money to his ex-wife, for their son."

"So what happened when Thomas claimed Martin's gun?" Felicia said, after I'd washed the knife and the cutting board.

"Told him no."

She grinned. "How'd he take that?"

"Said it was his by rights as next of kin. Said Martin had told him he was going to get rid of me, since I didn't get along with the rest of the crew. Thomas said he'd get a lawyer and sue me for the pay we'd gotten for the job."

Peter and Eli had come back inside. Peter put his arm around Felicia's shoulders. "What an ass," he said. "He has a lot of gall."

I wish I'd shot Thomas when I first had the idea. I didn't realize I'd said it out loud until they all swung their heads to look at me.

"Are you *crying?*" Felicia said. Seemed like all I did these days was cry, ever since I'd lost the baby. But I really, really didn't want to talk about it.

"That was a hard trip," I said instead. "The bandits who'd killed my friends had a good lead. They'd stopped to rape the women by the time I caught up. I had to kill all of them by myself. And we got to Corbin. Then I had to get back here." That return walk by myself had been the bleakest time of my life . . . at least to date. "And after that, I had to deal with an asshole."

There was silence from the others while they digested that.

"I think you're right. We should kill Thomas," Felicia said.

I wasn't sure if she was joking or serious. Peter and Eli smiled. Felicia and I didn't.

"If he gets elected, we'll have to move," I told Eli. I meant it.

"All the more reason," my half sister said.

I had to agree with her.

Eli said, "I will take care of him if I have to." He smiled again. "If my wife doesn't call dibs." He'd just learned that expression, and he loved to work it into the conversation.

People in Segundo Mexia and its surroundings tended to handle disputes one-on-one, sometimes with violence. As a country, Texoma was not that partial to law and order. Eli had taken to it like a duck to water, though it shocked him, too.

"I should have killed Thomas long ago. He's done dirty things to me as long as I've known him. But even in Texoma, I can't shoot a man for being a nasty piece of work and get away with it. There's got to be more to the story. If he draws on me, sure. If he tries to kill my sister, sure. If he slaps my mother in public? Absolutely. But not just because he makes me want to throw up."

Peter's eyes were wide as an owl's. "You can shoot someone here for slapping your mother? Oh, *boy*."

"I'm hungry," Felicia said. "Is the food ready? Can we eat while we talk about this?"

Trust Felicia to be practical.

"The meat should have simmered enough in thirty more minutes. I've got tortillas and beans plus some fresh tomatoes." I took the pot of beans out to join the meat over the fire. I wrapped the tortillas in aluminum foil to put in the coals for a quick warm-up right before we ate.

Though Peter looked a bit surprised at the menu, he'd have to learn to like it. My sister was all smiles. Felicia had grown up speaking Spanish and eating Mexican in Ciudad Juárez, south of the border. Even Eli loved spicy food. Me, I had been raised on anything cheap. The fresh tomatoes had come from my mother's garden. They couldn't be beat.

We sat at the picnic table with a big cold pitcher of tea and full plates. Even Peter seemed to enjoy the meat and beans and tomatoes, though he looked surprised a few times when he got a bite of pepper. He drank three glasses of tea. The heat was not so bad now that it was evening, and a breeze had come up the hill.

It felt good to be together. Two brothers, two sisters—well, half sisters—and a fine evening with plenty of food.

As we carried the dishes in to wash them, Felicia groaned with her hand to her stomach and said, "I may never eat again!" I smiled at her. She had a lot of growing to catch up on, though now she had left behind all traces of the child she'd appeared to be when I'd first met her. I could believe she was fifteen now.

Peter helped me with the dishes while Felicia took a quick shower. Eli stepped out to extinguish the fire.

I tried not to think any more about Thomas. A ball of fury

formed in my stomach every time I remembered the smirk on his face and his talk of people putting money behind him. Who would do that?

"Did you build your cabin yourself?" Felicia said, as if she knew I wanted to talk about something else.

At my request, she was sitting in the open doorway to comb her hair. I noticed that her hair was darker now that she wasn't in the sun all the time, almost black like mine, and a little wavy. I had gringo skin, and my hair was curly.

"Jackson and I built it together when I'd saved some money. I guess I was almost seventeen then. Didn't seem right for me to live with Mom and Jackson any longer." It had been a happy time for me. "I bought this land up here for almost nothing. Jackson helped with the building material and the construction."

"So you actually hammered all the nails and so on?" Felicia looked genuinely amazed.

"Yep. Jackson and Mom and I drew up the plans. Jackson showed me how to do the figuring on the raw material. We had a little help with the actual building of it."

My friend Dan Brick had helped, every hour he could get off from his folks' bakery. I'd been glad to have him. It was only later I learned Dan Brick had pictured living in this cabin with me. He hadn't been around since he'd realized that wasn't going to happen, after he saw Eli. I kind of missed him.

"You stopped in the middle of what you were saying," Felicia said.

She and Peter were staring at me. Eli had his back to us because he was reading a book we'd picked up at the secondhand bookstore in Fort Worth last time we'd passed through.

"I guess this thing with Thomas is spooking me," I said. My eyes lit on my husband, and he happened to look up at that moment.

"What's wrong, my darling?" he asked. When Eli was worried, he could get flowery.

"I guess it's time for me to go to bed," I said. "What about the rest of you?"

"I know I took a long nap, but I think I could get back to sleep," Peter said, yawning. Felicia nodded. "Me too."

"Tomorrow morning, I'm going to take Felicia to meet Chrissie and Mom," I told Eli. "Can you and Peter make sure we have enough wood for the cooking fire? Maybe take Peter by the hotel?" My stepfather owned the Antelope, the hotel on the town square. It had a bar and a restaurant. Peter had been there before, a day that had been pretty much a disaster. "I know Jackson would like to see Peter." I didn't say *again* because I didn't want to bring up memories.

"Of course," Eli said. He looked pleased at the idea of having Peter to himself.

Wood was not abundant around Segundo Mexia, where there weren't a lot of trees of any size. Eli didn't mind doing a lot of mundane tasks, but he didn't like to scrounge for fuel for the fire. He'd go into town and buy some from Franklin Wood. When people drifted into Segundo Mexia, sometimes they took new names to simplify their lives, and often those names had something to do with their means of living. Sometimes—often—they were escaping from trouble elsewhere.

CHAPTER THREE

The morning was less hot. We ate oatmeal for breakfast with raisins thrown in. Felicia and I did the dishes while Peter and Eli got ready to go. They both had their vests on.

I did my best not to make a face.

The people hereabouts would have cottoned to Eli much more quickly if he didn't wear the vest; it marked him out as different and made them anxious. If he only wore it when he was working, even. But the one time I'd brought it up, he'd let me know in no uncertain terms that leaving the vest at home was as out of the question as me leaving my guns at the cabin.

Peter and Eli were talking nonstop as they walked down the hill. I had to smile, watching them. They might not look that much alike, but anyone could tell they were brothers.

We took in the laundry I'd done the day before and folded it, and I swept out the cabin. Felicia kind of raised her eyebrows.

"We take turns," I said, warning her from starting any picture of me as a downtrodden doormat. "They're going to be gone for hours, you know." They'd have a lot of talking to do about family stuff.

"About losing the baby . . ." Felicia began.

"I don't want to talk about it. It was awful, it's done."

Felicia gave me a strange look, part understanding and part doubt. "I don't think that's all you feel about it. And how is Eli?"

"Not now," I said, and after a few minutes of silence, we were okay again. I asked Felicia if she wanted a sandwich, but she was still full from the late breakfast.

I strapped on my Colts, but there was no need to take the rifle.

"You always go armed?" Felicia said.

"As often as Eli puts on his vest." The difference was that people knew I wasn't going to shoot them without provocation. They weren't so sure about Eli's spells.

I brushed my own hair (outside) and put combs in it to hold it out of my face. Felicia asked me to help her braid her longer hair. I had it done real neatly in a jiffy. I tied a bow around the end to keep it in order. I felt sisterly.

Felicia beamed at herself in the bathroom mirror. "I'm really looking forward to meeting your mom," she said.

Felicia didn't remember her own mother, who had died of a fever when Felicia was a little tyke. I could tell she hoped somehow my mother would feel maternal toward her. I also knew such a possibility had never crossed my mother's mind. But there was someone else who was panting to meet Felicia, and in a couple of minutes, we were knocking on her door . . . even though it was open.

My neighbor Chrissie popped out immediately, with Emily Jane on her hip.

Chrissie was still pretty, though with three children in the past six years, she'd weathered some. She and her husband started their family early. Chrissie was just a year older than me—I'm twenty-one and a bit. Her husband, Lee, was away from sunup to sundown, working as a ranch hand.

Chrissie worked those hours, too, cooking and washing and watching the kids, in between going down the hill to do her shopping and attend the Catholic church. She also visited her folks and her brothers and sister. The past school year, nearly over, had been a golden time for her, both boys enrolled and only one baby to tend.

I introduced my half sister to Chrissie, who gave Felicia a very thorough once-over. "You're going to be taller than Lizbeth," she said. "I know you're happy to see your sister! I can't imagine living so far from my family."

"I am glad to see Lizbeth," Felicia agreed. "Where do your folks live, Chrissie?"

"Right yonder in town." Chrissie pointed downhill and to our right. "They're east of the square. I'm expecting the boys home from school in a while, but I have some time before then if you two can sit for a spell."

"Sure," I said. My mother would still be busy at the school, anyway. We followed her inside.

Chrissie had a floor of painted boards, a recent development. I'd had some lumber left over after we'd finished the new room, and I'd given the boards to Lee. He'd managed to get some more, and with this, he'd put in a floor. Chrissie was so proud. She'd painted it dark green with what was left over when her parents had painted their house. Lee had also gotten a couple of sheets of plywood to build a partition between the bed he shared with Chrissie and the kids' beds.

Chrissie forced Felicia and me to take the chairs, while she sat on the bed. We took turns holding the baby. Emily Jane was fair and plump—and calm, thank God. Emily could walk, but she preferred to sit in someone's lap, and she enjoyed being carried. Emily entertained herself now by pulling a lock of my hair straight and then letting it spring back into a corkscrew.

If it made the baby happy I was willing to put up with it.

Chrissie was delighted to talk to someone new, and she'd never met a stranger, just people who weren't her friends yet. She had a million questions for Felicia about living in a city, riding on trains and buses and in cars, and going to a large school—all experiences Chrissie had never had.

Felicia seemed to enjoy the conversation as much as Chrissie did. She answered every question she was asked in great detail. We drank lemonade, ate cookies, and enjoyed ourselves far longer than we'd planned. When Dellford and Rayford came pelting in from school, I realized we'd stayed a while and Chrissie had things to do.

Dellford and Rayford were very active boys, skinny and blond like their mother. Both of them had become better behaved since they'd started school. My mother didn't suffer bad behavior. After a day in the past when Dellford had saved my life with a well-thrown rock, I, too, had become active in teaching the boys how to be good citizens.

Someday when Lee was home, I'd see if he and Chrissie would let me give the boys a shooting lesson, see if either of them had any aptitude. Dellford and Rayford were fascinated by Eli, but neither of them showed any signs of having magical talent.

When the boys found out Felicia was training to be a grigori—if the tsar didn't bleed her dry in the meantime, but we didn't talk about that—they were fascinated by her. After a few minutes of their open-mouthed admiration and three thousand questions, Felicia gave me a quick and meaningful glance. We stood up to leave.

"Chrissie, we got to go. Since your boys are home, I guess my mom is cleaning up the school." I ruffled Dellford's hair. He very properly looked disgusted and made a face at me. We said our goodbyes. Chrissie hugged Felicia, startling her.

My half sister was silent as we made our way down the hill path. I wondered if she was thinking about her own childhood. Was there a difference between country poverty and city poverty? Mexican poverty and Texoman poverty? Probably not.

"Look!" Felicia pointed down at the town. "Is that normal?" We'd reached the halfway point and were still enough above the town to have a good view.

I followed the line of her arm. Like most communities, Segundo Mexia had grown up around a square. There was a small courthouse in the middle for when the circuit judge happened to visit. Below it on the ground floor were the jail and the county offices . . . or at least, that was where they'd been before, when this town had been in Texas and Texas had been part of the United States. There were benches and picnic tables arranged under the live oak trees.

The community celebrations took place on the square. The churches had potlucks here, and it was the site of the Christmas and Easter observances. In a far more rowdy celebration, the square hosted Texoma Independence Day.

At least 355 days out of the year, the square was quiet and often empty. Since so few people had cars, there weren't any pulled into the cracked parking slots. There might be a horse or two, because ranchers came into Segundo Mexia to shop. But most of the traffic was on foot, since the busiest stores were on or near the square.

Right now, it was the site of an ominous arrival.

Two large trucks with covered beds had come to screeching stops in front of my stepfather's Antelope Hotel.

"Where'd they come from?" I said.

"Not normal, I take it." Felicia's dark brows came together in a frown. "Who could be in them? What kind of trucks are those?"

There were so many things unusual about this that I couldn't begin to list them, but I could answer her question.

"Those are Dodge four-by-fours, Army transport trucks. At least, they used to belong to the Army." The US Army no longer existed. When the United States split up, whatever Army materiel had been stationed in the new countries belonged to those countries. The Britannia government tried to say all the munitions and vehicles were the property of Britannia. New America, Dixie, Texoma, and the Holy Russian Empire just laughed. (So did the parts of Canada and Mexico that had formerly belonged to the United States.)

Right now, no one was laughing.

One man climbed down from the cab of the lead vehicle.

From this distance, I couldn't hear his order, but clearly, there had been one. People in tan uniforms leaped from the rears of both vehicles and formed two rows.

The soldiers were all armed with rifles, clearly visible even at a distance. Ten issued from each truckbed. Three more descended from each cab.

"You're being invaded," Felicia said. "By twenty-six people."

"But . . . why?"

"Should we go down there? We don't know what's about to happen." Felicia looked doubtful.

"Nothing good." I stared down the hill in silence, thinking furiously.

"Eli and Peter are down there," I said, my mind made up. "Those gunnies are right in front of Jackson's hotel. My mother is cleaning up the schoolhouse two blocks away. Unless Jackson can make it over there, she's undefended."

Felicia straightened her shoulders. "Let's go."

As we began to hurry downslope, I heard a shot.

CHAPTER FOUR

I 'd been aiming my eyes down to keep my footing, but at the sound of gunfire, I risked a quick glance, though we were farther down and I couldn't get an overview.

Townspeople were swarming out of buildings, especially around the square, which was natural—but stupid. I also caught a glimpse of some wiser Segundo Mexians who were smart enough to exit the backs of the buildings, figuring they could make their way out of the area without being seen. Or shot. Or captured. Whatever those soldiers had come to do.

I was glad I'd strapped on my Colts, and I was also glad they were fully loaded, clean, and ready. I had enough bullets to kill every single one of the soldiers if I had to. And I was not standing alone. Felicia was an untrained but very powerful grigori.

Eli and Peter were quite capable of taking care of themselves if they avoided the gunfire, and they were wearing their vests, which was now a relief to me rather than an irritant.

I was only worried about my mother. I told myself that Jackson's first thought would be of her. Jackson did not ordinarily go armed. However, there was a shotgun loaded and ready behind the bar at the hotel. Jackson would grab it, first thing. If he could, he would head directly to Mom at the school.

If he could.

We'd reached level ground. We were on the path leading into town, the dust flying up at the thudding of our feet. We reached the backs of the first buildings and planted ourselves against the rear wall of Arnie's Feed and Seed.

"Where are we going?" Felicia asked.

"The school. It's a block north and two blocks west of the square."

"Where are Peter and Eli likely to be?"

"They've been gone for a few hours. I bet they've been wandering and talking and wandering some more. They'll have gotten the wood we needed. They may have gone by the hotel to see Jackson. That's where he is most of the time."

"The hotel we could see from the hill?"

"Yes, the Antelope. It's got a bar and six rooms upstairs, and it serves lunch and supper. Jackson runs all his businesses from there."

"So Jackson is a spider, and your mother's the fixed spot."

I nodded. Without discussion, we started running again. Felicia had put on slacks this morning, and she was wearing flat shoes. That helped a lot. Her braid flew around as she ran, like it was trying to lift her in the air.

We didn't meet another living soul until I spotted Agatha Hunter in her front yard, her rifle at her side. She was looking toward the square. She scarcely glanced at us as we pounded by. In the open door of their home, Agatha's husband, Donnie, sat in his homebuilt wheelchair, a shotgun across his lap.

"Easy death!" Donnie called to us.

"Easy death!" I called back. I felt proud to know them. They didn't know what the hell was happening, but they were ready to fight.

So far, we'd been lucky not to encounter any hostiles. Any moment, that could change. I heard more shots, two or three rifles firing at almost the same time. Unless I was catching an echo, these came from off the square and to the west . . . the direction of the school, the way we were headed.

"Not much farther," I told my sister. "Let's stop for a second."

We leaned against the side of the Food Shack, which sold tacos and hamburgers from eleven to seven. There were gaps in the planks, and I was sure that inside the shack, the owner could hear me gasping for breath.

"Earl, you okay? Is my mom in the school?" I said, in the lowest voice I could manage.

"Lizbeth, that you?"

"Yeah."

"Candle's in there, all right. She shut it up tight when we heard the first shot and the commotion."

"Thanks, Earl. Stay down."

"I plan on it."

Felicia and I crept around to the front of the Food Shack to eyeball the school for another minute. Surrounded by its large yard, it took up a whole block . . . though in this town, that wasn't saying much.

A rectangular one-story building constructed of rock and mortar, the school had first been a church. It had been erected right after the founding of Segundo Mexia. By the time the church's congregation had grown enough to need a larger building, there were enough children for a school. Ever since then, all the children in the area had learned the basics inside those four walls. I was lucky there'd been enough money to hire my mother as a teacher right after she'd qualified. She'd been there ever since.

The main school door faced west, opening onto a yard bare except for two redbud trees. The door was shut, and so were the windows, a sure sign my mother was battened down inside. Who'd close up the building in this hot weather? Even the bright curtains were drawn . . . except for a tiny gap. *Good for you, Mom*, I thought.

There wasn't a soul in sight. Nothing could be gained by hesitating any longer. Felicia and I exchanged a glance. Then we stepped out away from the shelter of the Food Shack and hurried across the street. "Mom," I said, tapping on the door. "It's Lizbeth! Let us in."

The second the bolt drew back and a slice of darkness appeared, Felicia and I slipped inside. My mother was behind the door. I threw my arms around her. I clung to her like I was the one who needed help.

"Lizbeth, I'm fine," Mom murmured. She held me close but not tight, giving me time to collect myself. "You must be Felicia," she said over my shoulder. She was using her teacher voice. "I'm Candle Skidder."

"Pleased to meet you," my half sister said politely.

I inhaled twice more and stepped back.

"What's happening out there?" My mother's dark eyes were wide with worry. "I heard a commotion from the direction of the square."

I told her about the trucks full of armed strangers in uniform. "We got no idea who they are or what they want," I said. "Their trucks are parked right outside of the Antelope."

"Jackson?" Mom said, trying to sound calm.

"We haven't seen him yet," I said.

"I haven't heard the shotgun," Mom said. "I opened the back windows so I could listen for it." She was keeping a hold of herself.

As we talked, Felicia was moving quietly from window to window, straightening and curling her fingers to make them flexible.

"Felicia isn't armed?" Mom said carefully.

"Oh, she's armed, all right," I said, loud enough for my sister to hear. "She doesn't need guns, though."

Mom gave me a blank look to let me know she didn't get the joke.

"Felicia is a grigori," I said. I had not been sure my mother wanted to hear about Felicia, so I hadn't told her much. "The school didn't realize she had the magic until a few months ago."

"They realized pretty quick after I killed my grandfather," Felicia muttered. She was standing to the side of one of the eastern windows, her head close to the little gap in the curtains. "They're coming," she said. Her hands twitched.

"Mom, lie down on the floor behind your desk," I said. The wooden desk wasn't much protection, but any was better than none.

Mom did exactly what I'd said. Candle Rose Skidder was good at many things, but fighting was not on the list. She would if she had to—she always did what she had to—but if Mom was fighting, it meant I was dead.

I moved to the other back window to see what Felicia had spotted. Two soldiers were approaching, both with rifles. They were prowling through the row of houses on the next street to the east. They were alert. There were patches on the shoulders of their khaki shirts, but I couldn't make them out from this distance.

"Those familiar?" I whispered.

Felicia shook her head. She raised her hand with her fingers folded to imitate a gun. Was I going to shoot them?

I considered. I could do it, of course, but the windows were closed, and I'd have to allow for the glass affecting my shot, which would be from an awkward angle. And the two soldiers (mercenaries? militia?) were at least ten feet apart, so one of them would have time to react. I tossed the idea when I thought about the noise. Shots would draw more of the soldiers. Too risky.

I waved a hand to get Felicia's attention. I raised my eyebrows to show I was asking a question. Then I held a finger to my lips. Then I drew a finger across my neck.

Felicia nodded with a little smile. Focusing through the slit in the curtains, she extended one hand, nodding gently as she felt her way through the spell. Our father, Oleg Karkarov, had told Felicia that all forms of magic were drawn from the same pot. Felicia might be a grigori like him or a witch like her mother. I wasn't sure it made a difference as I watched her work her magic.

Felicia's fingers opened and tightened, opened and tightened. The mercenary nearest Felicia, a man, paused. His free hand went to his throat. He opened his mouth to say something to his companion, but the words never got out. Felicia opened her fingers one final time and then clenched them in a fist. The man struggled to breathe, dropping his rifle. He turned white and crumpled to the ground. He didn't move again.

His companion, a tough woman in her forties, glanced over as he fell. For a second, she didn't believe her eyes. Then her mouth opened to yell. In that second, Felicia had begun repeating her spell much more rapidly. The woman struggled violently, swinging up her rifle to fire an SOS shot. She took a step closer to her fallen comrade, just close enough to the window to reach.

I flung up the window, reversed my Colt, and leaned out to slug her in the head before her finger could pull the trigger. She went down silently, but she was not dead.

"Finish," I said.

Felicia did.

I unlatched the back door and pulled in the woman by her booted feet as quickly as I could. Felicia began hauling in the man, but he was too heavy. My mother appeared out of nowhere and grabbed one foot while Felicia took the other, and together they dragged the body into the school. I took a final look around before I shut and locked the rear door.

My mother looked green around the gills. We'd stowed the bodies where they wouldn't be the first thing you saw if you opened the door. That was all we could manage; there aren't a lot of hiding places in a one-room school.

"Don't look at 'em, Mom," I said. "It's done." I was already worried about the drag marks we'd left in the dirt.

Felicia went to the front windows. "Someone's coming," she said quietly.

I was beside her before you could say Jack Robinson. "It's my stepfather," I said with relief. I unbolted the door and opened it a crack. Jackson broke into a trot. In seconds, he was in and looking around wildly for my mother. They came together like a magnet and a nail. He didn't say anything, and she didn't, either, but they didn't need to.

Jackson was more bulldoggish than handsome, but you always knew he was in the room. And he was a good thinker. He'd propped the shotgun against the wall carefully. After he'd reassured himself that my mother was all right, he noted the bodies lying up against the wall. When he didn't see bullet holes, he turned to my half sister.

"Jackson, this is Felicia," I said. "She came with Eli's brother on the train."

"Felicia," he said easily. "It's good to meet you. Where are Eli and Peter?"

"We don't know," Felicia said. "They left this morning to run errands, and we just came down from the cabin a few minutes ago."

"They dropped by the Antelope and ate lunch there," Jackson said. "I enjoyed their company." He paused. "And you haven't seen them since? Where were they going to get wood?"

"Trader Army's or Franklin's, I don't know which."

"They still wearing their vests?"

"Sure," I said.

"Might be good, might be bad," Jackson muttered.

"Why?" Felicia asked.

"They've got all their spell stuff with them, but they're marked out as grigoris," I said.

She shook her head at herself. "Of course."

"Did the mercenaries come into the Antelope?"

"I was already going out the back door, so I don't know," Jackson said. He grinned, but not like it was funny. He had to live with running away, because sometimes running was the smart thing to do. "My bartender and the desk clerk got out, too. I had to stay put in the stables for a while to avoid the patrols."

I crouched down to search the woman. My mother sat on one of the benches and looked away. Jackson helped by taking the second body.

"Dammit," I said.

The pockets were empty of identification. The woman was carrying a handkerchief, two bobby pins, and a comb. The man had a handkerchief, a picture of a young man, and a cross.

Their weapons were standard weapons, in use by the US Army when there had been a US Army. The woman wouldn't have been in the ranks then. A lot of things had changed besides the name of the country we lived in.

"I found something important in a dead man's shoe one time," Felicia said.

She crouched to untie the man's brown boots, but first she had to remove the canvas leggings. Felicia's mouth pursed when she found nothing but dirty socks. She set to work on the woman's feet but didn't have any luck.

"These are some thorough people," I remarked.

Jackson had watched Felicia work with a half smile on his face, while Mom had kept her eyes averted.

Jackson's muscles tensed. "Heads up," he said, almost in a whisper.

We all froze in place, Felicia and me crouched on the floor, my mother sitting on a bench, Jackson close to a window a yard from the man's body. He flattened himself against the wall. My mother started to slide off the bench to the floor, but he held up his hand, palm toward her. She settled back. Movement is eye-catching.

We all listened.

"Where'd they go?" a voice said. I figured it was a young man, and I figured he was standing just outside the fence around the yard of the schoolhouse. He wasn't making any attempt to be quiet. "All the people who live here?"

"They ran for their homes," said another man, who sounded older. "They got to figure out what's happening."

"You think they'll fight?" the younger one said hopefully.

The older man laughed, a relaxed chuckle. "You better hope not, Nick. These ain't city people, these are country people. They can shoot, and they're tough."

Damn straight. There was something about his voice, a little too loud and more than a little self-conscious. The older man suspected some of those "country people" might be listening . . . and ready.

"Where are Merle and Betty?" the younger man said. "Weren't we supposed to meet them here? This is the schoolhouse, sign says."

"I don't see hide nor hair of them," the older man said. "Maybe we'll see them back at the truck." He did not sound convinced of that. "Let's just mosey on." Definitely uneasy. Definitely thought someone was listening.

"We should wait a while longer," the younger man said. Jeez

Louise, the kid couldn't shut up. "Last time I saw them, they were walking between the buildings right east of here."

I drew a silent breath in, let it out just as quietly. My Colts were ready in my hands. *Easy death*, I thought, but the idea that now if I died, it would be in front of my mother . . . I got more and more tense. I could see Jackson was ready to leap to his feet.

But we all *waited*.

Even Felicia, who was strung like a bow, almost quivering. The power was building up inside her to an intolerable level. She smelled like Eli, like a grigori . . . like magic.

I had the same father. I had no magic skill, but I could smell it being used. And I could boost its use by a real Grigori. Maybe I could take a little bit off the top as well. Might be a good time to use that little talent. I reached out very slowly and laid my hand on her shoulder. Felicia shivered. I began drawing off some of the overload as evenly as I could manage. I hoped I wasn't blundering into something that would backfire. But after two minutes, my half sister could manage. She relaxed.

Sometimes I wondered why the Rasputin School required Felicia to finish the low-level grigori courses when it was obvious she had power running out her ears. But after something like this, I understood. Control was everything to a grigori. Control and focus.

"I guess they ain't coming," said the young man, and yawned.

I had gotten so intent on Felicia I had forgotten they were there. That was stupid.

"I guess not," the older soldier said.

In the distance, someone gave a shrill whistle.

"Back to the trucks," the older man said.

We listened as their footsteps faded away. And we all relaxed, but we stayed where we were until we heard the faint sound of the trucks starting up. They went south.

Jackson said, "I'll be back with the wagon," patted my mother on the shoulder, and left. He was moving fast.

"What?" Mom asked, bewildered. "Where's Jackson going?"

"We got to get the bodies out of here," I said, my voice as smooth and calm as I could get it. "Those soldiers are gonna come back, sooner or later. We got to get these two out of the town limits. Away from the school." At least there wasn't any blood.

"I think I can dig the hole," Felicia said. "I'll go with Jackson, too."

"You're an earth grigori?" I was pleased. She would be able to make a good living, though moving dirt around wasn't exciting.

"Nope. I'm like Felix," my sister said. She gave me a significant look with wide eyes. Then she shrugged. "But I can move some earth, too, like Eli can. Just not my best thing."

I tried to keep my face blank, but I was truly shocked.

Felix was a death grigori. He could pull the life out of someone . . . and he could also put it back in, though that was harder. Not the most comfortable man to be around.

I'd known my sister could kill silently (or loudly, for that matter), but I'd never realized that if she could kill that way, it was an unusual skill. Felix didn't have many friends. Felicia would also be more of a target once her power became known.

"That's why you're with Felix so much," I said.

Felicia's letters had let me know that in addition to the regular school classes, she was being specially tutored by the grumpy, thirty-ish Felix. Until now, I hadn't been able to figure that one out.

"We'll talk again. That sounds like your stepdad returning."

Felicia was right. The wagon rolled to a stop right outside the school. It behooved us to move quickly. We wanted as few eyes to see this as possible.

"Can you make the bodies lighter?" I asked.

My sister nodded. Her eyes closed, and all the emotion washed from her face. It was eerie. The man's body rose in the air, just a bit, and I took the shoulders. Mom rose off the bench and bent to lift the feet. She always responded to need, even when she was revolted by the task.

We were both surprised by the lightness of the body, and I'm sure Felicia noticed. She smiled proudly. I tilted my head toward my sister to tell my mother where credit was due.

In five more minutes, Jackson, Felicia, and I were in the wagon heading out into the low hills southeast of Segundo Mexia. Mom was finishing the end-of-term school cleanup she'd begun more than an hour ago.

Thanks to Felicia, Jackson and I buried the bodies in record time. Jackson dropped us off at the base of the hill, and he continued to the town stable to return the horses and the wagon, which belonged to the hotel.

I went up the hill in a hurry. I wanted to see Eli more than anything. Felicia hurried right behind me, just as anxious to lay eyes on Peter. I threw open the door to the cabin, sure the brothers would be inside.

But they weren't.

CHAPTER FIVE

F elicia and I talked about the situation till we had no more
to say.

Because she was fifteen, Felicia wanted to set out that
very minute. Reason (me) argued against that. Dark was closing in.
It was a bad night to be wandering around Segundo Mexia. People
were on edge and might shoot at anything. I told my sister all these
reasons to wait. Several times.

Felicia was trying not to be angry with me, but I could tell she
was unhappy. She was not good at hiding her feelings.

Tonight my half sister was just going to have to fume. She stalked
into the room she and Peter had used and shut the door behind her
very carefully.

I was too tired to eat anything. Felicia had been too angry.

I stripped, pulled on my old nightgown, and climbed into bed.
Though my body was exhausted, my mind was as crazy as a rat in a
cage. My body won, after a while.

I thought I heard Eli return at least three times that night. Each
time, I startled awake. Each time, I was wrong.

Felicia was more composed the next morning. But she didn't
want to talk, so I figured she was still angry. Being quiet suited me.
We ate some leftover tortillas and meat before making our way
down the hill. You'd better believe we were both keeping our eyes

open. This time, I carried my rifle in addition to my Colts, with extra ammo in a pouch, plus some food. We both had full canteens. Who knew what would happen?

"Nobody's out," Felicia said when we were halfway down the hill. "Normal?"

"Not hardly."

"Nobody" wasn't quite accurate. I could see a few people moving around. The patterns of the town were all upset, though. The few citizens who were on the streets were hurrying as fast as their legs could move, and they didn't pause to talk to each other.

"They're wondering if the soldiers will come back," Felicia said.

I nodded. "Let's start with Trader Army."

The sign on his door was turned to OPEN. The bell over the door jingled as we entered. Trader, his back to us, jumped just a little.

Trader's wife, Clarita, was sitting on a stool behind the till. No surprise there. They would want to be together after the scare of yesterday. Clarita was holding an ancient pistol, and she was ready to use it.

Army had lost an eye in the Mexican invasion after the US dissolved. The left side of his face was a mess of scars. But I never thought of it any longer until I introduced him to Felicia. Her face tightened for just a flicker. I was sure she had seen more shocking things.

Clarita was glad to see us; she'd always been a talkative and inquisitive kind of person. After Clarita had established my exact relationship to Felicia and learned that Felicia was fifteen and not married, I asked Trader what had happened in the square. None too soon—my half sister had started fidgeting from foot to foot.

"The first shot was one of them soldiers," Trader said.

"What was he shooting at?" I wanted Army to get to the body count, but there was no hurrying him.

"You're not going to believe this, but he shot Big Balls," Army said.

My mouth dropped open. (So did Felicia's, but for a different reason.)

"Big Balls is a pig. Was a pig," I told her hastily. "The butcher raised him from a piglet. Big was the meanest thing on four hooves, so he's no great loss, except to the butcher's pride." I turned back to Trader. "How'd that happen?"

"I don't know how Big got free—I suspect the little Hatcher girl, 'cause I spied her running for home. Be that as it may, Big charged the soldiers, and one of them shot at him. Big Balls was too mean to let that stop him. He kept on going and managed to get in a good bite before he died." Trader admired Big's attitude, and so did I.

At least the pig had gotten in a lick. That bite must have hurt like crazy. No one had ever seen a pig as large as Big Balls. After all the years he'd terrorized Segundo Mexia, Big Balls had died defending it.

"I guess the butcher will be eating good. I hope he saves me some bacon," I said, because Army was waiting for a comment. I just wanted him to *tell us what happened*.

"Did you see Eli and Peter?" Felicia said, making a huge effort to sound calm and casual.

"I did," Army said. "They'd been in here just before the trucks pulled up. They bought some wood, and there it is." He pointed to a bundle in a kind of leather sling. It would have been a bear to get up the hill for a regular person but not bad with Peter's and Eli's abilities.

"They heard the shots," Felicia suggested, trying to move Army along. But he was one of those people who wouldn't be hurried, I could have told her.

"Sure. And I was looking out the window and told them what was happening." Army nodded. "That Eli asked me to hold the wood till they got back, and then they were out the back door. I got my shotgun and went out after 'em." He glanced at his wife. "Clarita happened to be here, and I told her to lock the shop behind me."

Army's wife was the least excitable woman I'd ever met. Now she nodded, but her face did not show a bit of the alarm she must have felt.

Felicia took a deep breath. "So you ran out to see what was happening?" she said, her voice mild.

"Some of us did," Army said, nodding his shaggy head. "Some of us closed up shop and sat tight. I had to go see. It was crazy. All these soldiers in khaki, the bit one screaming. Frank Hacker went nuts because the bastard had killed his pig. Frank went on and on. He loved the pig, he had to be paid for the pig, and they better not take Big and eat him. The little Hatcher girl heard the shot, and she come back. She starts bawling, because she didn't expect anyone to _kill_ Big Balls."

I was going to seize Army by his shaggy gray hair and shake him. Enough about the damn pig.

"And then?" Felicia said, unable to wait any longer.

"The bitten soldier climbed back into the truck to lie down. One of the ones from the front of the truck had bandaged him up. The rest of them got their orders from the scrawny man. Off they went, this way and that."

"Did you hear the orders?" I put my hands on the counter and leaned over.

Possibly, Army got the point.

"Yes, I sure did! They were looking for a tall man with long light hair wearing a vest. They were supposed to shoot him on sight but in the leg or arm. He had to be alive. They'd load him up and take him with them."

There was a long moment of silence. Army and Clarita tactfully looked in other directions.

"Anybody say anything?" I asked, trying to sound casual and doing a real bad job of it.

"No one said anything," Army told me. "Emmie—that boy living at the stable?—he asked why they wanted this man, what had he done. The captain, or whatever he called himself, said he'd been reported as a threat to the peace."

"By who? And how come these hired hands had a right to follow those orders? For who to judge?"

"That he didn't say, and we weren't gonna ask." Army shrugged elaborately. "But we all wondered the same thing."

Clarita said, "They come back, best they not find who they're looking for."

Which was exactly what I had been thinking. If those soldiers, or mercenaries, or whatever they were, came back, the people of Segundo Mexia would start shooting, and the soldiers would shoot back. The loss would be more than one bad-tempered pig. And Eli would feel responsible.

He would be.

"I reckon you're right," I said, proud of sounding so calm. "Did Eli say what they were aiming to?"

They was gonna follow the soldiers when the trucks left."

I'd half turned to leave, and so had Felicia. We froze.

"You know this because . . . ?" I croaked.

"They told me to tell you."

"Thanks," I said. I bit off a few comments I wanted to make. "We got to get going, we've got a couple more places to stop."

"Keep the wood for us," I said over my shoulder. Then we were out the front door as fast as we could move without running. Felicia was about to explode.

When we'd walked for a minute, I said, "You have to get control."

Felicia took a deep breath. She nodded.

"We have to find Peter and Eli. We have to get them back," I said. There were a lot of things I didn't know, but I knew that. "If those soldiers catch Eli, Peter will be a bonus. They're searching for a magic worker."

"What do you mean?"

"They didn't know Eli's name. Someone told them a Grigori lived in Segundo Mexia." I suspected who "someone" might be.

Felicia nodded. "Yes, we got to find them. Eli's used to handling things, and Peter would have gone up like a firecracker when he heard the description." Felicia knew her Savarovs. "What first?"

"First, we learn *how* Eli and Peter set out to follow the soldiers."

"What do you mean?" Felicia asked again.

"I mean, they weren't going to run after them. Can't follow trucks that way. If they went on foot, they would only catch up with the Army trucks if the trucks stopped before too long. So I guess they went to find a truck or some horses."

Felicia nodded again. "Okay, makes sense. To the stable?"

"Yes." We were walking fast out of the square, heading north. The stable was one of the oldest buildings in town. I'd known the owner, John Seahorse, my whole life.

I am not as good a tracker as some others I know, but I have the basic skills. I had already picked out Eli's bootprints, which I knew well. The slightly smaller ones marching along with his must have been Peter's.

The tracks confirmed that Eli and Peter went to the stable and garage. When he'd purchased the building, John Seahorse owned all the rentable means of transportation in Segundo Mexia. He could work on cars and provide a place to keep them; he could house and take care of horses. John's young man, Emiliano, known as Emmie, was a talented mechanic. He was okay with horses, too, but John was better.

In the small yard in front of the stable, we found John Seahorse sitting on a barrel. Emmie was changing a bandage on John's right arm, and he was talking a blue streak in a jumble of English and Spanish. I didn't even try to piece it out. He glared at us as if we were the ones who'd shot his man. John smiled and winced at the same time.

"What happened to you?" I said.

"Just creased my arm," John said. He's a stoical kind of guy. I know for a fact, even a small bullet wound hurts. Those people who tell you you just have a flesh wound . . . they never had one.

"The soldiers or one of ours?"

"I don't think any of us fired a shot," John said. "Them soldiers popped off a few. When I came from behind the post office, they thought I was aiming to fire at them, but I just brought my rifle like you do when you hear someone shooting. I wish now I'd shot one of them."

"I hope it heals quickly," Felicia said, making an effort to be polite before she cut to the chase. "Did you see Eli and the guy with him? His brother Peter?"

"And you are?" As well as being stoical, John was blunt.

I introduced them. Felicia should have had a sign made for her chest that explained she was my half sister.

"Oh, right. Yes, I saw your husband," John said to me. "And the man with him, about Emmie's age? Looked like Eli's brother, for sure."

"That would be Peter," I said. "We're trying to find them. You got an idea?"

"Well, they're following those assholes in the trucks," John said, as if we should have known that already.

Of course, we should have. Eli wouldn't be able to resist finding out as much as he could about the weird and brief invasion.

But also, of course, they should have left word for us by some means more reliable than Trader Army. When I saw Eli again, we would be having some words.

"On foot? On horseback? In a car?" Felicia was too impatient.

"Yes," John Seahorse said.

"Which one?" she said, practically vibrating with need.

"Hold on to your hat, sister," John said. "They took the car. Same one you rented to go to the train station in Sweetwater."

The car was a sort of patchwork machine that did work, most of the time—but only because it had so much loving care. That was true of most vehicles in Segundo Mexia. My husband was no shade-tree mechanic like many of the townspeople.

"Is the car running well?" I asked, as if the answer was not important.

"Well as can be expected," John said.

Emiliano had finished his bandaging. John stood and looped his good arm around Emmie's neck. I could see how tired he was.

"You got two horses on hand?" I asked. I just barely caught the horror in my sister's expression. "You do know how to ride a horse?" I asked her.

"Yes, of course," Felicia said. "I mean, I *have*."

Good enough. "Get the horses, please," I told John. I paid him for two days with the horses, in advance.

"Emmie, saddle them up," John said. "Star and Birdie."

The boy was off in a flash. We could hear him talking to himself in Spanish while he saddled the horses.

I knew enough of the language to figure out what he was saying, and it wasn't complimentary to Eli. From the expression on Felicia's face (of course, she'd grown up speaking Spanish), I figured it was lucky Eli had left town after the little invasion. Emmie might have turned him over in a jiffy.

While we waited, I couldn't help but notice Felicia was as tense as a bowstring. It was the horseback riding.

"You could stay at the house in case they circle back," I offered. "That way, they'll know where I am."

"I'm coming." Felicia's jaw set even harder.

I didn't blame her.

CHAPTER SIX

Felicia

I was sure I could help Lizbeth. I'm not completely trained, but I'm effective. My one-on-one work with Felix taught me more than most grigoris ever know about taking life away—and sometimes restoring it.

My mother had been from a family of witches, the most notorious in Mexico. But Marina Dominguez had been unwise enough to elope with our father, a very low-level grigori (in fact, a bastard of Grigori Rasputin) named Oleg Karkarov.

Though I would like to sigh over their marriage as a great romance and imagine my mother and Oleg had been happy in their poverty because they were together, I knew different. Marina had stuck with my father until she died. However, that hadn't been very long, less than three years. My mother had caught a fever, the kind that runs through slums like dirty water. Though Father had sent word to Francisco Dominguez that his daughter was very ill, Grandfather had not responded. My mother had died. When my father hadn't been able to make ends meet during a bad patch when I was about four, he'd appealed to Francisco again and had been spurned again. My grandfather could have asked to raise me, and my father would have gladly let him. But Grandfather didn't. Only one of my aunts, Isabella, helped us out from time to time. She had to do it in secret. My other two aunts? My Dominguez uncle? Nope.

It hadn't been hard to kill them, at all.

Now Emiliano led two horses out of the stable. They were horribly big. I'd ridden a horse before. Once.

"I'll take that one," Lizbeth said, and John handed her the reins of the bay. "Felicia, you'll be fine with this one."

The dapple gray looked at me with mild inquiry, like she was waiting for someone to introduce us.

"What's her name?" I was trying not to look as scared as I was.

"Birdie," Lizbeth told me.

I tried not to look offended, because my sister was right. A horse named Birdie would be appropriate for me. Unless that was supposed to be funny? As in *This vicious horse has stomped three people to death, so let's name her something silly, like Birdie!*

I had to have help (from Lizbeth, since Emmie wasn't about to give me a hand). I couldn't have told you quite how it happened, but all of a sudden, I was on top of Birdie, holding the reins. I tried to look calm and relaxed.

Lizbeth had a few words to say to Star, the bay. She mounted the horse in one quick move. Then she maneuvered Star to Birdie's side to give me some tips about riding, but I couldn't pay much attention. I was up so high. On a horse.

John and Emmie went back into the dark recesses of the stable.

"You're determined to do this?" Lizbeth said.

"I am."

"All right, then. Let's go." And she sort of clicked her teeth with her tongue. Star strolled away like he had read her mind. And Birdie followed.

After a few minutes of terror, I relaxed. It was clear that Birdie would follow Star no matter what I did. That was really reassuring. And I didn't fall off. On the other hand, we didn't get above a steady walk. I opened my mouth to suggest we go a little faster, and then I shut it.

I hate horses. Riding a horse is like being on top of a building that's moving. But horses are like rattlesnakes, right? They exist. You have to be in the world with them. And they eat mice, I think (rattlesnakes, that is). So there's a good side.

But horses? Aside from giving people a faster way to get around, what purpose do they serve? I have to admit that to most Texomans or New Americans, that's enough.

Bump, bump, bump. Ouch, ouch, ouch. I decided to be angry at Peter and Eli for having taken the car, which I would have much preferred. That kept me going for a while.

When I could spare a second to think about something besides staying on top of damn Birdie, I was worried about my sister. If I was reading the signs right, she and Eli were not exactly pleased with each other. That was a real concern. They were married, and I'd invested a lot in the Savarov family. I was really fond of Alice and Lucy, Peter's sisters, and I got along with Veronika, his mother. As far as I knew, Lizbeth felt the same way, and besides, the Savarovs lived far away in San Diego. So Lizbeth's trouble must be with Eli personally. That was bad news.

After a while, I'd had all the thoughts about it that I could summon, so I went back to thinking about our trip and the means by which we were making it.

The horses.

At first, we simply followed the only road leading southeast out of Segundo Mexia. It might have been paved twenty years ago, but Texoma was poor, and it hadn't had any attention since then. On the other hand, Eli and Peter were easy to follow. Even I could see tracks in the dirt that had silted over the remains of the paving. Three tracks: the two big trucks and the car.

Lizbeth and I rode in silence. If I had my own concerns, she had hers.

After I got over being angry and worried, I spared some time to hate being dirty. I already felt sweaty and dusty, and I knew I smelled like a horse. That was something I shared with my sister; we both liked to be clean.

I had a hard time opening my canteen and taking a sip while I controlled the horse. Birdie made a real vigorous movement when the canteen had almost reached my lips, and the metal edge hit my gums painfully.

I called Birdie a terrible name. Then I gritted my teeth and kept following my sister.

At first, Lizbeth found it easy to follow the tire tracks. After an hour or so (which felt like eternity) of going south and somewhat east, we came to a crossroads. Unfortunately, this paving was clear of soil. Lizbeth circled around, trying to pick up the trail for a good ten minutes before she found it. I got to sit still. It was a great relief.

Once Lizbeth found the tire tracks again, we picked up speed. I had to bite the inside of my cheek, or I would have begged her to go slower. I held on for dear life and let Birdie have her head. Which she apparently wanted to stick up Star's rear.

I didn't fall off, and I didn't say anything.

On and on we rode, past groves of short trees, stands of cactus, and high, scrubby grass. Rocks littered the ground like pine cones in a forest, which made me worry about Birdie stepping on one. This landscape was much more barren than the area around Segundo Mexia. (I hadn't thought that was possible.) Segundo Mexia was like a garden compared to this.

From time to time, we'd see a stream or a watering hole. There was still water in them, which Lizbeth told me might not be the case later in the summer. We stopped to top up our canteens every time we'd had a bit to drink, and we let the horses have a drink, too. The air was so hot and dry I figured by the end of this very day, my nose and throat would be parched.

Lost in a wallow of misery and self-pity—there, I admitted it—I followed my capable sister through a strange land on a strange beast, hour after hour. The only thing stopping me from whining was my self-respect, and it was wearing thin.

Lizbeth didn't pay me any special attention, which I took as a compliment.

After a few eons of misery, I made myself take more interest in what was going on and less in how uncomfortable I was.

"Lizbeth," I said, and had to clear my throat not to croak. "Are we sure we're following the car tracks, not the truck tracks?"

"No," Lizbeth said. "I told you I'm not the best tracker in Segundo Mexia. But we are following tracks. If they belong to the trucks, that's what Eli and Peter will be following, too. And if it's Eli and Peter's car, so much the better."

"We don't know who we'll find first?"

She nodded, her eyes on the ground. "That is the case," she said.

It had never occurred to me that my sister wouldn't be the best at anything she undertook. I didn't know whether to be heartened or dismayed. But I did realize I needed to be very alert. We might be stumbling upon the wrong party.

While Lizbeth was focused on tracking, someone hostile might be right behind that clump of sage. Wouldn't do if that came as a big surprise.

The day went better after that because I had a purpose. I had to pay attention, I had to be sharp, I had to let Lizbeth be free to do what I couldn't do. I got to know Birdie a little better, and the ride became a bit smoother. My thighs were going to be screaming if I ever managed to get off this horse, but I decided to look on this as learning a new skill. I wondered fleetingly how many of my fellow students at the Rasputin School for Grigoris could ride a horse.

Always, I reminded myself to look around me, because that was my job. So I saw the smoke ahead before my sister did.

"Lizbeth!" I hissed.

She looked up immediately. We stopped moving. I guessed our horses were looking, too. The terrain had gotten more and more uneven. The hills were really hills now, not mounds. Sometimes they were rocky outcrops with only scrub brush here and there, and sometimes they were covered with trees, which grew thick but not tall. We were following the trucks—and the car—through a pass between two of these hills, of the heavily wooded variety.

"Huh," she said, very quietly. "At least we don't have to look for tracks anymore. I think that's smoke from a vehicle. We got to be real careful."

I didn't know how to be more careful on a *hulking great horse*. I felt as visible as a girl could be.

Taking advantage of any rise in the ground or clump of brush, we worked our way closer to the smoke. I did not know how to ride sneaky.

When we got near enough to smell the burning, Lizbeth swung down off Star. I looked at the ground, which seemed so very far away. I was scared to try it, but I needed to pee, besides the whole goal of finding out what had happened.

Then my sister was at my side, whispering instructions to me. Slowly and painfully, I followed them, descending ungracefully from the living mountain. If Lizbeth hadn't been there to catch me, I would have hit the ground. None of my leg muscles wanted to work right. For a minute, I clung to the saddle and panted. After that, I felt very sore, but my legs would hold me up.

Leading the horses by the reins, we moved slowly through the pass, staying as close to the trees as possible. No one yelled or shot at us. Lizbeth was taut as a wire, so I was, too. We came out of the short pass and walked gently uphill to stand at the crest of a low swell. From where we stood, the ground dropped mildly into a crescent-moon shape.

There was a burning car on this downslope. It was the rental car from the stables. Lizbeth caught her breath sharply, but that was the only sound she made. I wanted to howl, but I was sure there was some reason I should keep quiet.

The car had flipped over on its roof, like a beetle on its back. The doors had sprung open. So had the trunk, just a bit. The car's interior was charred, and the metal was blackened. The fire was almost out. The smoke trailing up into the blue sky was just a wisp of what must have been a good blaze. I shuddered. I had to know.

I tensed myself to leap forward, but Lizbeth grabbed hold of my arm. "No," she hissed. "Might be a trap."

"What if they're in there?" I hissed back.

"Then they're dead," she said. "We can't help 'em." Lizbeth said this as calmly as if it were the answer to two plus two.

My sister was being logical. I had to struggle with my impulse to scream. "Is this because you're sure they're dead?" I said hatefully.

"This is because I got sense," she said, not looking at me.

I took a deep breath. I said, "Sorry."

"Let's circle around to see if we can find anything else," Lizbeth suggested.

We began to move like crabs, sideways. I understood we were trying to gain the right angle to see if anyone was in the cab of the car. My breath started coming really fast.

"Shhhh," Lizbeth whispered. "Shhhh."

I got myself under control in a few seconds, and we moved again.

There was no charred figure in the driver's seat. Or in the passenger's. The trunk was open about an inch, probably from the impact.

I was about to tell my sister how relieved I was when I saw tears rolling down her cheeks. It seemed inconceivable to me that the dreaded Gunnie Rose would cry when she *didn't* find the body of her grigori. I covered her grubby hand with my own, which was equally dirty. We gathered ourselves for a couple of minutes. I may have cried a little myself.

Lizbeth stared blankly into the distance while she thought. I was so glad to stay on the ground for a moment longer that I let her think, though I had a hundred questions.

"We'll finish circling the car to see if we can find any tracks," Lizbeth said at last, keeping her voice low. "Since they're not in the car, they walked away. Or they were carried away. But there will be footprints. Or wheel marks."

"We haven't seen any," I said, very cautiously. There was probably some error in my thinking that Lizbeth would correct. "We haven't gone all the way around. And we haven't looked in the trunk."

There it was, lying in the air between us.

Lizbeth closed her eyes for a second. She said, "No, we haven't looked in the trunk."

I opened my mouth to say, *I don't think they could both fit in there*, but I shut it again before the words came out. And then I snapped.

I was in motion before I knew it, on my feet and running. There was a strangled noise from my sister behind me, but I kept on going down to the smoking car. I seized the trunk lid and yanked down with everything I had.

I hadn't foreseen two things: how hot the metal was and that the trunk lid might give way with little resistance.

Me and my burned hands staggered back. I landed on my rear, staring into the cavity of the trunk, so I had a close-up view as the body inside flopped to the ground.

Somehow my sister was kneeling beside me, her arm around my shoulders. We stared at the dead woman who'd been folded in the trunk around a spare tire. She had cooked rather than burned, since the trunk lid had protected the body somewhat from the flames. It was ghastly, and it smelled awful, and it was very close.

I turned aside to throw up. Lizbeth gagged a time or two but kept her stomach contents inside.

"You know her?" I asked when I could talk.

"Yes. That's Lotsee. She's the wife of a Comanche I know. I met her a couple of times."

"You're friends with the man?"

"Well . . . not enemies."

When we had gotten control of our stomachs, we had a closer look. Lotsee was wearing a flowered skirt, a man's blue shirt, and some moccasins. Her jewelry, a necklace and a bracelet, was still on her. Her black hair, now charred in spots, had been braided.

"She was shot before she went in the trunk," I said. I pointed at the bloody spot on her upper chest.

"We need to straighten her out," Lizbeth said.

I would rather have done anything than touch the woman's body. I'd lost all my gumption. I said, "All right."

We pulled Lotsee free of the car and carried her out of the depression, putting her in the shade of a tree. Lizbeth straightened the woman's clothes and crossed her arms on her chest. I cast a look around and spotted some wildflowers, which I picked and put at her hands. This felt silly, but if Lizbeth thought we had to make the body look cared for, I would help.

Lizbeth gave a satisfied nod, as if this was the best we could be expected to do. We took some steps away to talk, like our conversation might bother the dead woman.

"So, looks like Eli and Peter met up with some Comanches before the wreck, or maybe Lotsee was foraging on her own. Our two guys didn't have guns. This woman was shot by someone else. She must have been dead or dying. They decided to bring her along with them. I have no idea why she was in the trunk. Since your mad dash to the car, we know this area wasn't booby-trapped. Somehow they ended up wrecking in this hollow. And the car caught fire. Or was set on fire."

"And they left in a hurry."

"They would have been worried the car might blow up," Lizbeth said. "Either the fire was too intense to rescue Lotsee, or they knew she was already dead."

"That all makes sense to me," I said.

Our own tracks stood out pretty clearly. I circled the car. I found no other footprints. Lizbeth did the same. We looked at each other, baffled.

"Maybe they airlifted out of here," Lizbeth said. "So no one could follow them."

Including us.

"Airlifted?" I'd never heard that term.

"Like you did when you helped with the bodies. Sometimes Eli floats himself for fun. I bet Peter can do it, too."

"Oh, I've seen that!"

When they'd been taking two prisoners to the Rasputin School, the group of grigoris who'd come to rescue me from a bad situation (though I'd already rescued myself) had floated the prisoners to the school rather than having to keep hold of them.

"So we'll have to widen the search to pick up their trail," Lizbeth said. "They had to come down somewhere. Let's get the horses."

When I climbed back up on Birdie—with help from Lizbeth—

every muscle in my lower half screamed at me. I ignored the pain. I had to last through the day, no matter what. If we had to keep going tomorrow . . . maybe something would happen to the horses during the night? *Oh, no, poor Birdie! That lion just jumped out of the brush and ate her!*

Birdie swung her head around and looked at me, and I felt guilty. "Sorry," I muttered. Lizbeth gave me exactly the same look Birdie had.

To my huge relief, we found two sets of footprints on our widened second circle around the burned car. We began following this new set of tracks.

When we saw dark spots in the sandy soil, I said, "What's that?"

"Blood," Lizbeth said. After that, we didn't speak for a long time.

I wasn't *really* hoping it was Eli's blood instead of Peter's. But I was. Probably a similar, but opposite, hope was in Lizbeth's head. At the next large hill—about an hour after finding the car—we came to a clump of trees arching over high green grasses. I figured there'd be a pool of water close by, and there was.

We stopped so our horses could drink and graze a little. Lizbeth helped me down, but I did better this time. I walked around to stretch every muscle I had below my waist.

Peter and Eli had stopped, too.

"That's from the tail of Eli's shirt," Lizbeth said. She'd hopped off her horse and bent to examine the scrap on the ground. The bloodstained scrap. "He tore it off to use as a bandage. Or Peter did." She closed her eyes for just a second and took a deep breath. "We should eat something."

Neither of us actually felt like eating the food Lizbeth had brought. But we did, and we refilled our canteens, though the water was anything but clear.

After that, we went onward. This was the day that would never end.

CHAPTER SEVEN

Lizbeth

Felicia was swaying in the saddle. If we had to keep this up for another day, I didn't know if she could do it. I gave my sister a silent round of applause for staying on the horse and not complaining. That was all I had the heart to do.

I'd been thinking of the day I'd met Lotsee, wife of Standing Still. Usually, you got the English translation of the name (Standing Still's name was something completely different in Comanche), but Lotsee hadn't had enough of our language for that. I'd been in a gully trying to stanch the bleeding from a knife cut on my leg when she'd happened on me. I recognized her as Standing Still's wife, since I'd seen her walking behind him when they'd been in Segundo Mexia bringing some meat to the Antelope. Jackson bought game from Standing Still pretty frequently.

While Standing Still talked to Jackson, I'd had a kind of sign language/speech conversation with his wife. There'd been something agreeable about the woman, something in her eagerness to talk to me that day. I'd liked her. And when Lotsee had found me bleeding, she'd been a very practical helper. I might owe my leg to her help, or even my life.

Ordinarily, a body was a body to me, but since we had had a bit of time, I had wanted to do right by Lotsee.

I kept my eyes on the ground. My thoughts kept running over the same images: the wrecked car (for which I'd have to pay John Seahorse), the charred corpse of Lotsee, the blood on the ground and on the rag. I needed to concentrate on one thing, but my head was buzzing.

We went around the steep hills, since our guys would not have tried to climb them if they could avoid it. So far, I'd been able to pick up their trail.

After maybe two hot, sweaty hours, I was looking so hard at the ground immediately around my horse's hooves, when all of a sudden, right ahead of us, there was no more ground. We were on top of a low bluff, looking down some twenty feet at moving water. The fall would have been fatal, at least to Star and quite possibly to me.

"Oh, my God, I'm sorry!" Felicia was beside me, her eyes wide and her voice loud. "I was following you in a trance, I guess. What is this?"

"The Brazos River," I said, when my heart stopped thudding so loudly.

I turned my horse left, seeing a path downhill where the bank was just above the water. The horses drank again, while I filled our canteens. This time, Felicia got down without help.

I knelt and bent over so far I thought I might pitch into the river. I rinsed off my face and my arms.

"Can Peter swim?" I asked, as I stood up before I could give way to temptation and lower myself into the water.

"I have no idea," Felicia said. "It's never come up."

She hobbled to the river, took off her shoes, pulled up her slacks, and scooted forward enough to dangle her feet in the water. Her expression was so blissful that I pulled off my boots to join her.

"Wish I had some binoculars," I said, peering across the water. "I could see if their footprints continue on the other side."

"I think I see something," Felicia said. "I think I see where they sat down."

I stood and took a couple of cautious steps through the water. It might drop off closer to the middle of the river, but it was only a couple of feet deep close to the bank. Yes, I could see their footprints resume on the other side, barefoot for a few paces. Then a spot where the grass was matted down.

That was where they'd sat to put on their boots. Two butt-sized scuffs in the dead leaves and dust.

I heard barking in the distance.

"Felicia, keep an eye out for dog packs," I said. "I got to keep looking at the tracks."

"Dog packs?"

"Yeah. They're always hunting."

So many people had died in the flu epidemic. Others had taken off during the drought. Lacking food to feed themselves and their families, they'd left their dogs and cats behind them. Now those abandoned dogs formed packs and hunted down whatever they could find to eat. Sometimes that was cats, sometimes lone dogs, sometimes calves or grown cows, sometimes people. This was a hungry country.

"Why don't Peter and Eli stay *put*?" Felicia said, sounding really savage.

"Because they're following something they think is mighty important," I said. I sounded just as unhappy as I felt. "Those soldiers better be up to something real bad."

"They should have assumed we'd follow them," Felicia said. "They have to know that we're coming. Why the hell don't they just wait for us?"

I agreed with her a hundred percent. "We'll have to catch up with them to find out."

Probably, Eli and Peter could both swim. It was a short paddle across. The Brazos was narrow here, thirty feet or less.

I was not a good swimmer. And I had never crossed a river on a horse. I couldn't see another choice, though. I remounted, tying my boot laces and looping them around my neck. After taking a deep breath, I guided Star down to the water's edge.

"Okay," I said out loud. "Here goes." I made the chucking noise to tell him to go forward.

Star obliged.

"Hey!" Felicia yelled, but I didn't have the nerve to take my eyes off the surface of the water. She must have scrambled back into her saddle on her own, because the next thing I knew, Birdie's head was close enough for me to pat if I'd been so inclined.

Before I had time to worry, Star was climbing the gentle slope of the other bank. My legs were dripping wet, but I was safe. I kept on going a few yards to be sure Birdie and Felicia had room to scramble up behind us. I heard Felicia cursing in Spanish. I smiled for the first time that day.

"It feels good to be wet," Felicia said, when we were side by side. She was making a big effort to pretend she hadn't been terrified.

"It does," I agreed. "The horses did well." That was as close as I was prepared to get to saying they'd saved our bacon.

I began looking for tracks.

I found more blood.

My heart sank. This was not just a spot or a dash. "Felicia," I said, and she and Birdie came to see.

Felicia didn't speak for a minute. Then she said, "That's bad."

I nodded.

I was more careful than ever when I looked for more tracks,

which were getting hard to follow. The angle of the sun was not ideal, the ground was rocky, and the mountain cedar was taking over the landscape.

"What is that dark green bush?" Felicia said, after we'd scoured around for a few minutes. "It's everywhere."

"It's called mountain cedar, but it isn't," I said. I was looking at each blade of grass or weed or little depression in the soil. I was struggling, trying not to give in to my overwhelming uncertainty.

"Then what is it?"

"Some kind of juniper, Mom says," I told Felicia absently. "No real mountains around here or any cedar. Doesn't agree with a lot of people, gives them a runny nose and headaches."

As if her body had heard my words, Felicia sneezed violently.

"There are male and female trees, Mom says." I was just talking to keep my mouth busy so I wouldn't bawl or curse. The blood had been a serious amount.

Felicia gave me a sour look before she sneezed again. The violence of it bent her over. She stayed bent. "Look," she said, and her voice was calm in a scary way. I urged Star to Birdie's side, and I looked where her gaze was fixed.

There were drag marks leading into the nearest clump of mountain cedar.

I was off of Star before I knew what I was doing, handing my reins to my sister. Then I burrowed into the dense growth like a mole into sand. I found the body straightaway.

"It's not them." I realized I'd whispered, and I raised the volume. "Not them, Felicia!"

"This girl is too scared to answer," replied a dry male voice.

I drew with my left hand. With my right, I parted the bushes, just wide enough to see. My sister was regarding a Comanche man astride a black horse. Her hands were drawn up to her middle. She was ready to kill him. I wasn't sure he understood that. He believed Felicia was too frightened to speak.

"Standing Still, my sister can kill you. She is ready to do it," I warned him. I pushed out of the bushes, careful to step out facing him.

"This girl is your sister?" the Comanche said, seeming only mildly interested. "She doesn't have weapons, Kills with Guns."

Kills with Guns? I had an Indian name? "My sister does a different kind of killing. Her hands don't have to hold guns to kill people."

He shrugged. Standing Still was probably in his early thirties. He was thin and scarred. His horse was in better shape than he was. "Death is death. I found the body of my wife. You treated Lotsee with respect. Who is it you have found?"

"Not Eli or Peter. Not my husband or his brother. That's who we've been tracking." I wanted to be sure Felicia understood.

Felicia's eyes widened for a moment but then focused on Standing Still. She was staying at the ready. It made sense. She didn't know him and he'd snuck up on her.

"This is Standing Still, Felicia," I said. "He belongs to the Comanche tribe. He was Lotsee's husband. He sells game to the inn sometimes. I know him."

"Do you?" Her voice had an eerie kind of timbre.

"Stand *down*," I said. "He didn't have anything to do with all this."

"I would like to know what 'all this' is," Standing Still said.

Felicia relaxed just a fraction.

"I will tell you what happened yesterday in Segundo Mexia," I said.

I did, trying to keep my story orderly.

"So we are trying to find out where our men are. We found Lotsee's body in the car our men had borrowed. She had been shot. Eli and Peter don't carry guns." I paused, wanting to be sure Standing Still registered this point. "We tracked our men here. Now I've found a dead man in these bushes," I said. "He's one of the soldiers."

"So you think these soldiers shot Lotsee, and your men put her in the car to take her to get help."

"Yes."

I couldn't claim to know much about the Comanche, since they were secretive about their own ways. I didn't blame them. If I'd busted out of a land where I'd been forced to go, I would be careful in my dealings with white folks, too.

Standing Still was off his horse and pushing through the mountain cedar before I could say another word.

"Kills with Guns?" Felicia said, one dark eyebrow going up.

I shrugged. "Could be worse."

Standing Still reappeared. Though his face was not one I could read easily, I stepped back.

Felicia moved her horse away a little.

"We have been tracking the blood for an hour or two," I said, trying to get Standing Still to focus on the moment. "And hoping our own men are alive."

"The tall man with the light hair, he is your man? With pictures on his skin?"

I nodded toward Felicia. "And his brother is hers."

Standing Still gave my half sister a comprehensive once-over. "What can she do?"

"She can kill with magic." I wanted to be sure he knew both of us were not defenseless.

"I have seen these men," he said.

"In the uniforms."

"Yes, they have a camp about two miles from here. Close to Armadillo."

I'd heard of the town, though I couldn't recall why. The feeling attached to the name wasn't good.

"How big is Armadillo?" I asked, to give myself time to think.

"Like your town," Standing Still said.

"Small? Not on the railroad?"

He nodded.

"Who's the law there?"

"There's a sheriff, woman named Joanie Lang."

The breath froze in my lungs.

From far away, I heard Felicia say, "What's the matter with you, Lizbeth?"

CHAPTER EIGHT

Lizbeth

"She's big trouble," I said.

Felicia gaped at me, and even Standing Still seemed surprised.

"Let's go," I said. There was no way around it. "Now that we're pretty sure they're headed to Armadillo, we can make haste. Which way?"

Standing Still pointed west. "An hour's ride that way."

I helped Felicia remount, and Standing Still hadn't left by the time I was in the saddle.

"You coming with us?" I asked, not sure how I felt about it.

"My wife is dead and dishonored. I burned her body. I will kill whoever did this to Lotsee."

I nodded. I would expect nothing else.

He nodded, and then he was gone to get his horse, tethered somewhere around.

"Not a big chat person," Felicia offered.

I shook my head.

Felicia kept trying to start up a talk because she wanted to know what was wrong with me. I kept being quiet.

I'd met Joanie Lang when she'd been a gunnie for Sammy Philbert out of Dallas. She was maybe thirty then. I was sixteen. I'd been working for Tarken and Martin out of Segundo Mexia. They'd been out of town, I'd been free, and she'd needed another gun.

I'd thought she was incredible. Just short of six feet tall with cotton-blond hair and dark brown eyes, Joanie Lang—a great shot and second in command of Sammy's team—had been everything I'd wanted to be.

Our job was receiving some cargo from a wagon master close to the railroad tracks in Dallas.

We'd been ambushed. The bullets had flown. I couldn't remember what the cargo was or why someone else had wanted it so much. But they had, enough for people to die. Joanie and Sammy had gotten trapped behind a row of empty barrels, and I'd thrown myself behind there, too.

"We're going to circle around behind those sonsabitches," Sammy had said. He was in his forties, as weathered as an old boot.

Of course, I'd followed Sammy and Joanie.

Sammy had already been wounded in the thigh. He was barely holding on. We'd stepped over one body from his crew and another one severely wounded. I'd stopped to tie a tourniquet, using my bandanna. I remembered the impatience on Joanie's face, the scorn she'd given Sammy, whose face was waxy with pain.

That should have been a huge clue to me.

In the end, we did get behind the bandits, and we did kill at least four of them. The rest of them ran. My head was as big as a balloon.

I'd spent that night with Joanie. I understood a little bit then—and a lot when I got older—that Joanie should have been tending to her crew rather than giving in to the surge of lust that follows a lot of shooting. During that night, her crew member, the one I'd tied the tourniquet on, died. Sammy lived, but he was never the same.

The sex had been intense, probably because I hadn't had any before; but by the next morning, I'd realized I was pretty much a woman who liked a man in bed.

I'd gotten word about Joanie from time to time. Her reputation got more and more serious. She seemed to have no trouble replacing crew members who died in the course of the job—which was good, because there were a lot of them. The last I'd heard, Joanie had been hired by Iron Hand, the top-level security company on our continent.

I couldn't imagine how a face-off between Joanie and me would end.

Seemed as though I might find out.

"Lizbeth, talk to me!"

Felicia must have been saying this for some time. Her voice was real loud and cranky.

"I'm not talking now," I said. "Later."

Because she was smart, Felicia shut up and concentrated on riding her horse.

Standing Still had not returned by the time we knew we'd reached our goal.

I could smell the camp before I could see it: latrines, horses, motors, cooking, unwashed people. Felicia made a face to show what she thought of the odor, though I figured by now, we ourselves were plenty gamy. We dismounted, Felicia very stiffly. She had to lean against Birdie for a minute or two before she could walk. I was proud of her for not complaining.

"They must have sentries up," I whispered.

Felicia nodded. She closed her eyes to listen harder.

We didn't have a plan. We needed more information. Felicia made some signs with her hands and threw a pinch of something from her pocket into the air. I found that interesting. "So they can't hear our horses," she whispered, as we tethered them.

I should have asked a question about that, but I didn't.

Felicia and I worked our way into a clump of mountain cedar taller than us. Through a slow and prickly process, we crawled to the other side of it, where we had a good view of the camp. I began counting the soldiers.

"Forty?" Felicia breathed.

"At least."

There were four neat rows of tents, ten each row. I figured two soldiers per tent. A larger tent and an in-between-size tent had been pitched to the right of the enlisted ones. I figured the biggest tent was for the commander, the somewhat smaller one for the higher-ranking officers. I hoped one of those tents held Eli and Peter.

Felicia tapped my arm and pointed. Okay. Probably the one with the soldier standing behind it. The front flaps were visible to the camp, but prisoners might sneak out the back.

Who were these people? What was a military outfit doing in the middle of nothing?

I put my head down, exhausted beyond my reckoning. Losing the baby had weakened my body. I was sure I would get back to my old self, but I was still low on strength. I forced myself to return my attention to the camp. Information was always good.

The mercenaries were wearing the familiar khaki uniforms. They all wore sidearms, and a few of them, I assumed the ones on duty, carried rifles.

Weapons were expensive. The trucks, the horses (there were at least twenty tethered behind the commander's tent). Food for the humans and fodder for the horses. It all added up to a lot of money. Who was funding this?

Two cooks were stirring pots over campfires. A third butchered a cow on a rickety table nearby. Tame meat, not game meat. Also expensive.

The off-duty soldiers were strewn around, playing a dice game, polishing their boots, washing their uniforms. Eight of them were on sentry duty in a ring around the camp, facing outward. The sentries were really alert. That spoke to their training. But weren't they too close to the camp to be effective?

Dammit, what do they think is going to happen? I fumed. *They should be lax and careless, out in the middle of nowhere.*

"Keep real still," said a low voice behind me.

In one move, I pulled out my knife and pivoted, pushing up, to stab the man leaning through the cedars behind me. He'd opened his mouth to yell to the others, but the only thing that came out of his throat was blood. Felicia caught him as he crumpled to the ground, easing him prone quietly, while I snatched his rifle from his hands and rolled over to avoid being spattered.

"Well done," Felicia whispered, after we'd caught our breath.

"Why didn't we hear him?" I whispered back.

We were squatting by the body, our heads close together. The bleeding had almost stopped.

"I don't know. That's the kind of thing that gets you killed."

Okay, she hadn't picked up on my sarcasm. "Do you think it might be the spell you used to silence the horses?" I said, through gritted teeth.

"Oh. Crap. Well, all right, I screwed up. Look!" Felicia pointed. "That's the guy who came to your house, isn't it?"

Thomas Carter had emerged from the second-largest tent, rocking back on his heels with a satisfied expression. His suspenders and trousers were part of the uniform, as were the boots, but he only wore an undershirt above the waist. The tent flap moved behind him, and a woman emerged in full rig. She was taller than Thomas.

I said a word that seldom passed my lips. Felicia's eyes widened. "Joanie Lang," I told my sister. "I got bad history with her."

Felicia's mouth folded into a pucker. "So it's worse," she said. "Thomas hates you, and she does, too."

"In a nutshell." It didn't take an Iron Hand detective to see they'd been having sex. I couldn't imagine Joanie had found it fun, since she primarily liked women (short, dark-haired women). But Thomas's posture was proud when he glanced at her. If he'd been a rooster, he would have crowed.

Joanie's face was blank when she looked at him.

"I would as soon have sex with a dog," I told Felicia.

"Which one repels you more?" She was trying not to smile.

"Both of them," I said.

"Who do we kill first?" she asked.

I was *aching* to kill Thomas. I was indifferent about Joanie. I'd opened my mouth to tell Felicia this when a newcomer rode into the scene.

Prancing up on a gorgeous black horse was a man in a fancier uniform. He had more insignias on his arms, a different hat, and even medals. His neat white beard and trimmed white hair said that he looked in the mirror a lot. The newcomer dismounted easily, walked over to Joanie, and glanced from her to Thomas with clear disapproval.

"Condition of the prisoners?" White Hair asked Joanie.

"Stopped the bleeding on the younger one, sir," she said.

"Bring them out," White Hair said.

Thomas went over to the sentry standing in front of one of the small tents and said a few words. He was grinning, as if he had a treat in store.

I noticed the guard looked over Thomas's shoulder to Joanie for confirmation. She nodded.

I grabbed Felicia's arm as Eli and Peter stumbled out of the tent, their guard holding open the tent flap. Their hands were bound behind them. Both of them looked rough—dirty, smoky, blood-stained. I could see bruises on Eli's face, and one of Peter's eyes was swollen shut. Seeing them injured pumped strength through me like nothing else would have.

White Hair took all this in and looked even more displeased.

"Lang, when I told you we needed magic practitioners and you told me you knew of some, I thought you understood I would not want them impaired or mistreated." He gave Joanie a severe look. Seemed Thomas was her dog to heel. Joanie looked bored.

"They resisted. Kneel, you two," Thomas ordered, loudly enough that we could hear.

Kneeling is hard when you can't use your arms.

Eli managed pretty well, but Peter would have pitched forward if Eli hadn't twisted awkwardly to grab his brother's sleeve.

"So do we get up and start the killing? Or what?" I whispered.

Felicia glared at the ground. Her hands were literally twitching. "I'm ready when you are."

"As long as you know I'm killing Thomas."

"The sooner the better, sister." She'd dropped the *half*, too.

The soldiers were gathering around, hoping for entertainment. Two of them were positioned between me and Thomas. Every muscle I had was bidding me to leap up and start shooting. I was on a knee, the other foot planted to push me upright. A gun was in my right hand, the other in my left, and my rifle was ready on the ground beside me. All the soldiers had to do was *move*. Not that I minded shooting them, but Thomas needed to go first.

Thomas was enjoying his last few minutes of life. He loved having Eli and Peter at his mercy. He loved having an audience. Without warning, he took a step forward and backhanded Eli with everything he had in him. The men between us shifted. *Yes!*

I stood and fired in one smooth move. My bullet hit Thomas in the side of his head, spraying blood. Thomas collapsed to the ground in the limp way of the dead.

And then I was crouched down beside my sister, concealed.

Eli had fallen to his side from the blow. He lay still, but I could tell all his muscles were tense. He was trying to figure out what was happening before he moved again. Peter, still on his knees, had hunched his head over, trying to be smaller.

Everyone else was in motion.

It really was like I'd kicked over an anthill.

The mercenaries were running in all directions. Their rifles were in their hands. Joanie yelled "Take cover!" while they were already doing it. She grabbed a rifle from the nearest sentry. She crouched, partly protected by a wagon, her eyes darting around as she tried to locate the shooter.

"That was impulsive," Felicia said. She sounded calm.

"I didn't know I was going to do it until I did it," I said.

"Let's wait just a second," she said, even more calmly. I knew from her tone that I had sounded pretty excited.

When nothing else happened, silence fell.

Joanie stared at our particular clump of mountain cedar and began to raise her rifle.

White Hair raised his hand.

"I don't know who fired that shot," he said loudly (so that "who" could hear). "I'm sure you had your reasons. I am not heartsick at the loss of Thomas."

"That's what happens when you're an asshole," Felicia whispered. "This is a flowery bastard, huh?"

"If that is all you wanted, the death of Thomas, you can back away and leave. I will not pursue. But if there is anything else here you want, we have issues." The flowery bastard had drawn his sidearm. Near as I could tell, it was a Colt, like mine but newer, probably Army-issue.

"Then we have issues, because I want two other things," I muttered.

"I don't have to see them," Felicia said, mostly to herself. "I know where they are." She closed her eyes and began to whisper.

I felt the swim of magic around me. I stayed absolutely still.

To my relief—since we were so outnumbered—the soldiers began to crumple where they stood . . . even Joanie, who held out seconds longer than anyone.

Soon there was only one man standing.

Felicia let Flowery Bastard stay upright. That was a surprise.

Peter, still kneeling, was looking at this all happen in amazement, as well he might.

"I'm so proud of you," I told my sister, with all my heart. "Are they dead?" I really couldn't tell. They hadn't flopped like shot people.

"Let's go see," Felicia said, grabbing up the sentry's rifle.

We stood. I slung my rifle over my shoulder but kept my guns in my hands. We parted the branches to step out onto the campground.

Flowery Bastard was for sure startled when we appeared, maybe because we were young women or maybe because he'd thought we'd be somebody else. But he got even stiffer in the back and looked stern, just as if he meant to give us two younguns a good talking to. Only my upheld hand (and possibly the gun in it) stopped him from chiding us.

I stood guard while my sister untied Peter's wrists and helped him to his feet. They embraced for what seemed like a very long time. I was pretty sure Felicia was actually holding him up.

"Could you have a look at Eli?" I said, with what I thought was a lot of restraint.

Peter and Felicia let go of each other and practically leaped over to my husband.

"He's coming around," Felicia said.

Being knocked unconscious is not good for your head. He might be addled for a while. "Sister, can you keep watch on this officer while I see to him?" I said.

"Sure thing," Felicia said, assuming a sentry position. As I passed her, she whispered, "Just to let you know, I'm kind of fried from expending that much energy."

I did need to know that. Flowery did not.

Eli had definitely taken a beating. His nose might be broken. But his pride had taken the worst punch. To be taken prisoner by normal people . . . that wouldn't suit Eli at all.

His eyes opened as I was touching his face, and his hand shot up to grip my wrist in an unfriendly way.

"It's me," I said, trying to sound soothing, which was not something I did well. "We got you. Peter's okay." I moved behind my husband to take the rope off his wrists.

"Here I am," Peter said helpfully. "That guy hit you pretty hard. But Lizbeth shot him dead."

"Good," Eli said. His voice sounded raspy. "Thanks, wife of mine." He didn't sound thankful. He sounded pissed off.

I noticed that Peter's arm was bound with Eli's shirttail, which explained the scrap we'd found while we were following them.

"Peter, what happened?" Felicia said, noticing his wound at the same moment.

"The Indian woman stabbed me," Peter said. "She'd been shot. She thought we were the ones who'd done it. She didn't have much English, and we couldn't seem to get it across to her that we wanted to help."

"We found the car," I said.

"Did the poor woman live?" Peter looked anxious, especially for someone who'd gotten stabbed by the poor woman. He pulled away from Felicia and stood on his own.

"No."

Peter's face sagged. "We tried. She was bleeding pretty bad when we came upon her."

"Her name was Lotsee. I knew her a little. Her husband's looking for you, too. You put her in the trunk because she stabbed you?" I had not been able to figure that out.

"We had to. We didn't know what she'd do next," Eli said. He closed his eyes for a moment. He'd had as much as he could take for now, it was clear. He said, "I want to sit up."

Peter and I each grabbed an arm and pulled, and then Eli was sitting. He looked kind of dizzy for a long moment, and then his face cleared.

"Okay, that's better," Eli said. "At least . . . it will be."

Felicia was still keeping an eye on Flowery, but she'd eased closer to us. "We better get out of here," she said. "I don't know who's going to show up. Maybe more soldiers, maybe Comanches, maybe some townspeople from Armadillo, which ought to be over that rise to the north of camp. We don't know how they felt about these people being here."

"Good idea," Peter said. "Can you stand, Eli?"

"Of course," Eli said. After we'd hauled him to his feet, he bent over and vomited.

I looked at Felicia and raised an eyebrow. *What next?* She shrugged, very slightly.

We'd been ignoring Flowery Bastard, though we'd been keeping an eye on him. Now he drew himself up and said, "You have just killed a whole squadron of my people. I don't regret Thomas Carter's death, but these other soldiers were good people. Lang was a staunch woman, too. A good officer."

"A good officer cares about the welfare of her soldiers," I said. Just like a good gun crew leader tends to her crew. "Joanie never gave a damn about what happened to the people she hired. And why was Thomas Carter here, in uniform? He was supposed to be running for sheriff in Segundo Mexia."

This, too, Flowery was willing to tell us. I was getting suspicious that he was cooperating this much. He expected to live.

"We were doing a campaign sweep through this territory," he said.

That was really vague.

"Carter came to tell Sergeant Lang that he knew of a magician in Segundo Mexia. As it happens, my superior had told me to look out for a magician, just recently. So I sent a cadre of soldiers to see if they could find this 'grigori.' That's what they call 'em in the HRE. My men were clever enough to make sure he would follow them from town, and then we caught 'em."

Eli had followed the trucks from Segundo Mexia because he wanted to find out where they'd come from and what they intended. No cleverness on the part of the soldiers was required. In fact, if the older soldier of the two (the ones we hadn't killed) had decided to risk his life, they might have caught Felicia. (They would have been so sorry.)

I thought, *I bet that was the sentry I killed. I bet he had some magic in him. He knew we were in the schoolhouse, he knew magic could kill him, and he left. Maybe he knew Eli and Peter were following, too. But because Felicia spelled us, he didn't know how dangerous we two were today.*

All this ran through my mind as quick as a roadrunner. I pushed it back to think over later. Instead, I picked up on another suspicious thread in the conversation.

"A recruiting drive for the New America Army? I didn't know there was such a thing. I guess you need a course in map reading, brother. This is Texoma, by at least twenty miles."

"I must have made a mistake," Officer Flowery said mildly. "The people of Armadillo didn't seem to mind. Not one of them raised the issue."

Of course not. An infusion of hungry and horny soldiers with money to spend? A place as poor as Armadillo?

"Besides," I said, "that's not a New America patch you got on your shoulder. That's a new one. Who pays your soldiers?"

"What soldiers?" he said, bitter. He pointedly looked from body to body.

He was dodging the question with a lot of agility.

I might have thought of more questions to ask, since he was being so forthright, but Felicia had another pony to ride.

"Because you needed magic, suddenly it became all right to hire or steal a magician?" she said. "Convenient. Besides, I don't think you represent New America at all. People in New America, they hate magic and people who practice it."

"Now, look, girl," Flowery began. He'd had enough of us, and he wanted us to know it.

"No, you look. Who do you think killed all these people around you?"

"They're dead?" Apparently, he'd been hoping they were just unconscious. (Though I wondered why the power of someone who could knock that many people to the ground would be any less scary, if that had been the case.) "All my people? I alone left standing?"

"Boo-hoo. Give a look, mister." Felicia spread her hands in a *be my guest* gesture.

The older man looked from face to face of the fallen. "Are they . . . are they *crying*?"

I glanced at the soldiers lying near us. Tears of blood ran from their eyes, following whichever path led down, depending on the way they'd fallen. Was my sister being *artistic*? I couldn't believe the Rasputin School had ever let her off their grounds.

At this strange and tense moment, Standing Still rode into the encampment. Even under his circumstances, Flowery stiffened at the sight. Never any love lost between any white army and Comanches . . . or any other tribe.

"You have been busy," Standing Still said to Felicia and me. He glanced at Eli and Peter. "And you got your men back."

"Thank you for your help," I said.

"I have killed all the sentries. Aside from the one you took down."

"Thank you." I didn't know how to phrase the next sentence. "Are you satisfied with your vengeance?"

"I need the life of the leader."

Felicia and I looked at each other. She didn't quite shrug, but I got the drift. "His life is yours, Standing Still," I told the Comanche.

"Why do I owe this man anything?" Flowery said. He was finally worried, since to him, a male Comanche was much more threatening than me or Felicia. Even with the bodies of his troops on the ground around him.

"Your soldiers shot his wife," I said. "These all of them?"

"Yes, all of them," Flowery said.

He was lying. According to my math, there were some not present or accounted for. We needed to get out of here before any more arrived. Felicia was out of magical juice, Eli and Peter could barely stand, and I was low on ammo.

Standing Still had had time to look around him. "They are weeping," he said, matter-of-factly.

"Penitence for their part in having harmed your wife," Felicia told him, not skipping a beat. The white-haired guy wasn't the only one who could be flowery.

I went to the hitching line and looked over the horses quickly, picking the two bays that looked best cared for. I didn't want the fancy black horse, he was too recognizable. I saddled the bays up and led them over to where Eli was standing.

"Here!" Flowery said. "Do you really intend to hand me over to this Indian?"

"Yes," I said. I didn't owe him any explanation. He was just wasting my time. He kept talking, but I quit listening.

It was a job getting Eli in the saddle, but we managed. While Standing Still tied Flowery's hands together and remounted to lead him away, Felicia bravely went to retrieve our horses. She led Star and Birdie to us as if she were leading dragons. Peter gave Felicia a boost and mounted his own horse easily.

Before we left, I thought to check the biggest two tents for communications, and I found some kind of field telephone or telegraph in the largest tent.

It was too cumbersome to carry away. I pried off the cover with a handy screwdriver and scooped handfuls of dirty sand inside. Also, I cut out some wires with my knife and stuffed them into my pocket to throw away.

Standing Still and his hostage—and the beautiful black horse— were gone when I ran out of the tent.

I started the ride home in much better spirits than I'd set out. Peter seemed grateful to be free and happy to be reunited with Felicia, who was feeling all sassy and proud of herself.

My husband wasn't feeling any of those things.

CHAPTER NINE

Felicia

I didn't mind the horse so much now that Peter was riding, too. Also, his horse didn't have a name, so that made Birdie superior. Peter seemed to want to be quiet for a while, so I kept my peace. By and by, he felt like talking.

"It wasn't a smart impulse to follow them," Peter admitted, as his opening statement.

I waited.

"But we both decided to do that," Peter said. "Eli wanted to find out who was threatening his town, and I thought we'd have an adventure. So off we went. We did tell that man in the store."

"We got the message, but only when we stopped in there to find out if you'd been seen," I said, trying to sound as if I hadn't been angry.

"Oh. Well . . ." Peter was clearly trying not to explain anymore. If I had to guess, I'd imagine he would have said something along the lines of *Eli said we had to go right away*.

"And?" I prompted.

"At first, the tracks of the trucks were easy to follow. Those places where the road had dirt sifting across made it simple."

I nodded.

"But I guess you knew that. When they left the road, it got harder. You know that, too."

"Yes," I said, so I wouldn't have to nod. Now that I was thinking about it . . . though I was full of energy from the dead, I'd expended a huge amount of magic. And I was aching all over from the horse.

"Then we found the Indian woman by the side of the trail we were following. They'd shot her."

"Did you wonder why they'd left her there?" I said, as neutrally as I could.

"No. She was hurt bad. We tried to help her. But she didn't understand that. She roused enough to stab me, so we put her in the trunk . . ."

"Put an injured woman in the trunk of the car."

Peter's jaw got all tight. "Well, she had *stabbed* me! If we'd put her in the backseat and she'd come to while we were moving, she might have tried to stab Eli." But Peter looked ashamed, as well he ought. I assumed they'd taken her knife away. What was she going to attack them with? Her fingernails?

"Did you ever think that woman might have been left in the path of whoever was following them, by the soldiers? To slow the followers down?"

Peter sighed. I almost felt sorry for him. But not really.

"I can't speak for Eli, but I didn't think of that at all. It was all a mistake," he admitted. "Given what happened afterward."

"So tell me about that?" *Let's move along, shall we?* Ahead of us, Eli and Lizbeth were riding side by side silently. Lizbeth was glancing over at Eli pretty frequently, checking on how he was doing with his pounded head, I guess.

"Then we got ambushed by some of the soldiers. They set a trap. One of them stayed behind to see what happened."

"Explosives?"

"Ah . . . yes. Not a big charge. Under something, but right on the track we were following."

"And it blew up under the car?"

"We must have just clipped it. Because instead of blowing up the whole car, it knocked us sideways off the track and into that sort of bowl in the ground." Peter shook his head. "It's amazing, really, that neither of us was hurt worse. But the poor woman . . ."

I started to say, *Oh, the one in the trunk?* but I didn't want to grind it in anymore. I was sure she had been left in their path, to slow them down so the soldiers would have time to plant the explosives. The soldiers might have hoped, but hadn't known for sure, that the people following them were the very people they'd been sent to find.

Peter nodded miserably. "We knew we had to get out of there as soon as possible, though we were pretty wobbly."

Of course.

"We hurried as much as we could, not knowing how many of them there were or if they'd left a guard to see how the booby trap turned out. We were quick enough to catch up with one."

"You crossed the river."

"We swam, but my bleeding got worse after that. We had to stop for a minute or two. But we found him, and I killed him."

"How?"

"Oh, I took a pinch from this pocket . . ." Peter reached to where the pocket should have been on his grigori vest, if he'd had it on. He looked stricken. "Our vests!"

"Lizbeth grabbed them up from the commandant's tent," I said, because I had some mercy. "So you took a pinch of something from your pocket?"

"And I tossed it at him and said the right word. It was supposed to look like a gunshot."

"It did. And you hid him in the bushes."

"I didn't think we'd ever get him out of sight. You saw him?"

"Yes." *We thought it would be one of you.* "So when did they catch you?"

Peter closed his eyes and squinched them up, like someone had suddenly pinched him.

"Eli was feeling worse from the car accident, dizzy, but he wouldn't turn back," he said. "I was trying to help him, but I was also trying to watch for signs of the camp and stop the bleeding on my arm. That was one thing too many. When I smelled the camp, we slowed down. But we'd passed a sentry without seeing him, and he came up behind us."

I remembered how shocked Lizbeth and I had been. Only the speed of her response had saved us from the same thing happening.

Maybe it hadn't been my spell to quiet the horses. Maybe the sentry himself had had some kind of spell to cause him to make no noise. If so, it had died with him. "Do you remember what he looked like?" I asked.

Peter gave me an uncertain look. "Ah . . . average height, clean-shaven, light hair?"

That was the description of a lot of people, but it definitely matched the man my sister had killed. "He surprised us, too. Lizbeth got him," I said.

Peter sighed in a defeated kind of way. "Good for her. I sure didn't have a chance. He had a gun on us and had called the others before I could react. Eli was really flagging at that point."

We rode in silence for a while. I was biting my lip not to ask Peter why, if they were so disabled, they hadn't simply waited for us to show up.

But my resolution collapsed.

"Why didn't you just wait till we got to you?" I said, trying to keep my voice low. "Why the hell did you keep going?"

And here was the moment I learned a lot.

"Eli said we had to keep going," Peter said, just as quietly. "I knew you'd come, I knew you'd help, and I knew we'd be much stronger when you'd found us. But he wasn't listening, and I couldn't let him go on by himself."

"Did he think Lizbeth wouldn't come after him?"

"I don't know what he thought," Peter said miserably.

After that, we were silent for quite a while. I couldn't pat Peter on the head and tell him it would all be okay, because that wasn't what I believed. Also, he was old enough to realize that himself. Sometimes I understood that Peter was older than me, but sometimes it was all too easy to forget.

I could only imagine what my half sister must be thinking and feeling. She'd been pretty much bulldozed into actually marrying Eli by his mother, abetted by Eli himself.

Lizbeth wouldn't have gone along with the bulldozing unless she'd loved Eli. I knew they'd been happy. But the bloom seemed to be off the rose, as my roommate Anna would have put it.

I knew Lizbeth had read some romance novels, and maybe (not being very experienced with the real thing) she figured that was how it was supposed to be? Love ever after? Hard to imagine her believing something so unrealistic, knowing her as I did.

At the moment, Eli's pride was smarting; didn't need a crystal ball or a Russian seer to tell that. He'd gone after the mysterious militia to defend his new hometown and get the goods on the interlopers—and maybe as a great adventure to entertain his visiting little brother. Instead, his brother had gotten stabbed, Eli had wrecked a car and banged his head, they'd been captured and beaten and humiliated, and he'd been hit in the head again.

His rescue had come from the efforts of his wife and her little sister.

I wasn't surprised he was being an asshole, because all men are. They can't help it, apparently. But I was sorry Eli was running true to form.

Lizbeth deserved a man who appreciated her. If she'd been any less persistent and efficient, Eli would still be in jail in the Holy Russian Empire. Instead, she'd rescued him again when he'd been tied up in a tent. The mysterious militia would have had Eli *and* Peter.

So. Screw his pride.

One of my classmates at the Grigori Rasputin School had referred to a session of blunt truth telling as a "come-to-Jesus moment." Eli needed to come to Jesus. Right now.

We rode into Segundo Mexia very late that night. We should have stopped to camp, but knowing beds were waiting for us at the cabin, it was impossible to think of a night on the ground with any stoicism.

Maybe I was giving my feelings to the others.

We stopped off at the stables to put the horses in their stalls. Lucky there were two empty ones for our appropriated horses. We did our best to be quiet so we wouldn't disturb John Seahorse and Emiliano, who lived in a house at right angles to the stables and garage. Peter and Lizbeth did some quick horse tending while I sat on a fencepost outside, not even pretending I wanted to help.

Eli waited with me. I could tell he was in pain, but I was not a healer.

"Tomorrow we'll have to tell John Seahorse about the car," Eli said, his voice heavy with weariness. It was the first thing he had said in hours.

"If we give him the new horses, that'll offset some of what we owe," Lizbeth said as she trudged out of the stable, Peter staggering behind her. "If I'd thought of it, we could have brought more back."

Eli did not respond.

As we set off home through the silent town and up the hill, all I could think of was a bath and the bed. The others had to be dreaming of the same thing.

When we were inside the four walls and happy to be there, Lizbeth said, "Eli in the bathroom first, so I can doctor him before he goes to bed."

Eli did not protest. He fetched a pair of loose pajama pants. He was in the bathroom with the water running before you could say Jack Robinson. Lizbeth listened at the door in case he passed out. I got out all her first-aid stuff. I have to admit, he showered quickly and was out in record time.

I told Peter to go next so we could take care of him, too. It was the most unselfish thing I had ever done.

Lizbeth and I looked at all Eli's injuries. "You might have a cracked rib," she said. "I think your nose is going to hurt for a few days, so don't touch it if you can help it. Maybe your cheekbone is fractured. How does your head feel?"

"I'm dizzy," he admitted.

There wasn't much we could do for any of that, other than wrap his ribs. The bruises on his face and torso had developed just fine during the ride back. Lizbeth had some pills for pain that she'd hoarded from a long-ago injury, and she let Eli have one.

Peter's stab wound was more of a long slice rather than a deep cut. It was lucky (for Peter) that Lotsee had been shot, so her blow was weak.

Lizbeth dabbed the wound with iodine while Peter bit his lip. She had a powder she used to aid clotting, and she sprinkled it liberally on the wound and bound it tightly with strips from a clean but ancient sheet. She told Peter not to get that arm wet the next day and to leave the bandage on for two days . . . the same advice I would have given.

Eli had been hovering around while Peter was being doctored on.

"Go to bed, Eli," Lizbeth said, standing with an effort. "I'll be in as soon as I'm clean."

Without another word, my brother-in-law vanished into their bedroom, his eyelids drooping. Peter gave me a kiss on the cheek before doing the same. Lizbeth and I looked at each other.

"You had the harder day," I said. "You go first."

Lizbeth looked surprised. "Thanks. I hope your butt isn't too sore tomorrow. You want a pill?"

"I'll go to sleep just fine without one," I told her.

Lizbeth kept her nightgown on a hook in the bathroom, and she came out smelling much better and looking like a pretty girl. A pretty girl who was dead on her feet.

"I'm sorry," I said, then was sorry for the impulse when Lizbeth looked away.

She shrugged. "It'll work or it won't," she said. "He misses San Diego, and his family, and all his grigori friends. I think he even misses Felix."

"Hard to imagine," I muttered.

Felix, my mentor, now married to Eli's sister, was a great grigori with immense talent. Too bad he had no charm to match that.

A smile crossed her face so quickly I almost missed it.

By the time I had scrubbed myself clean with the very little remaining hot water—which felt like heaven—and brushed my teeth, the house was silent. I closed my eyes and listened with my ears and with my mind, but there were no enemies within the scope of my physical or magical ability. That was refreshing, because I didn't believe I could win a fight with a baby opossum, let alone an armed soldier. My butt was too sore. And my thighs. And my back.

At least I didn't smell like a horse any longer.

We might have all snored the roof off, for all I knew.

CHAPTER TEN

Lizbeth

I was the first one up the next morning, which was no big surprise. I wanted some time to myself, so I didn't make bacon. The smell would have had them all sitting at the table drooling. Instead, I made another pot of oatmeal with some dewberries I'd picked the week before and kept sugared in the refrigerator.

I carried my guns, my rifle, the sentry's rifle, and all my cleaning materials out to the picnic table after I'd covered the rough surface with an old blanket. I wanted peace. Cleaning the tools of my trade was the best way I knew to achieve that. I took the bench facing the cabin so I could watch for our guests.

It was so calm and quiet. The temperature climbed quickly, but a gentle breeze was blowing. Chrissie's children were quiet.

I let my thoughts drift as I cleaned and polished. The smell of the Hoppe's was like perfume to me.

I was relieved Thomas was dead. He'd been a thorn in my side for years. Thomas had believed whoever funded the militia would back his run for sheriff. He'd been so cocky about it. I wondered how he'd happened to connect with Joanie, who had been doubling as sheriff of her town and a militia officer. Why?

Could there be other bands of this militia in Texoma?

We should have asked more questions. Too late for that.

Finally, I came to the thing I did not want to think about but had to.

Eli and me. I feared he didn't believe it was working out. He had known going into our marriage that I'd never be a proper Princess Savarova. He'd been clear on that, on who I was. I knew he had seen me, understood my life.

That having been said, that he had seen me entirely, I thought we had a chance. He had to have realized what our life here would be. It was a poor place and very mistrustful of Russians in general and grigoris in specific. He had overcome that, had made a place for himself here, and we had a pleasant life. At least I'd thought so.

It seemed Eli did not find our life so pleasant.

What more could he want? I asked myself that over and over. We had enough food, enough money, a house with electricity and running water, no debt, and work to do. This was all I'd ever imagined. But now I knew Eli had imagined something else.

Eli had had a very different life in San Diego. His having to leave it behind had not been any doing of mine, at least not directly. I couldn't magically wish his father had *not* been an asshole and traitor who'd ruined his family's chances of advancement in the Holy Russian Empire. I hadn't been one of the political adversaries who'd falsely put Eli in jail.

Maybe Eli's discontent with our life is his dad's ambition coming out in him, I thought. I hoped that was not so. After I'd considered that (I had to admit I found it probable), my mind wandered through the past.

Eli and Peter had both disliked their father, but could Eli harbor some resentment against me for his father's death? Vladimir Savarov had come to Segundo Mexia to kill me . . . and he would have taken out Peter, too, if I hadn't intervened. I shrugged. It was done.

By now, both Colts were clean and shining. I laid them aside. I'd started to work on the rifle by the time Eli came out of our cabin with a bowl of oatmeal in his hands. He settled himself on the bench across from me. He'd left the cabin door open. It was getting hotter.

I continued working on my old Winchester, a gift from my grandfather. The familiar work soothed me.

"Are you mad at me for killing your father?" I said, before I even knew my mouth had opened.

Eli thought about it. "No," he said. His voice was firm and steady.

"Then what?" I put down the rifle and folded my hands in front of me. I gave him my full attention.

My husband sat silent for a moment or two.

I braced for a blow.

Eli delivered it.

"I have to go back to San Diego," he said. "I got an urgent telegram."

"This is because . . . why? Because I lost the baby?"

"How can you even think that?" Eli said, sounding genuinely shocked. "Of course not."

Because you never wept. You never told me you were sorry. You never asked me how I felt. I could not say these things. He must know them already.

"When will you leave?" I said. My voice sounded like another person's, someone who was far away. I didn't take my gaze from him. I would not look away. As long as I concentrated on Eli, I would not cry.

"I need to leave as soon as I can. I'll take Peter with me." He thought hard about what to say next. "Your sister, she's the most talented grigori we've seen in years. She's completely willing to use her power."

Willing and eager, I agreed silently.

"But she's called to court to give the tsar her blood. You don't like it, and Felix is always grousing about it."

"You've been hearing from Felix." I'd seen letters in Eli's hand, but I'd figured they were from one of his family members. While I absorbed that, I said, "Felix always grouses." My brain was racing around like a spring colt.

"Yes," Eli said, surprised. "I never thought you'd be interested. I know you don't like him."

I could feel my mouth purse up. Even though Felix was married to Lucy, Eli's sister, he'd always loved Eli. Had the telegram been from Felix? He'd do anything to get Eli back to San Diego. "So Felix says you need to return quick. How come?"

"Not Felix," Eli said, standing. "And I don't want to explain until I know more."

I stared at the man I'd thought I knew. I believed he was leaving me. Though I also knew that was kind of crazy, it was the only way I could figure it. He was going away without telling me exactly where or what he was going to do. And it was urgent. And he was taking his brother. And leaving my sister.

My husband had been making these plans while he'd been sharing my bed, eating the food I'd cooked, working alongside me, having sex with me.

My breath went out in a gasp.

"You're a traitor like your father," I said, finally looking at him. I hardened my face against him.

Eli was staring at me as if I'd shot him. What had he expected? "No," he protested. "You don't understand."

But I did. "If you stay, I'll kill you."

Hardly aware of what I was doing, I gathered up my guns and my cleaning things and went inside to our bedroom.

My sister followed me.

I sat on the edge of the bed . . . our bed . . . my bed. Felicia sat beside me, our arms touching. We didn't speak for what seemed like an hour. During that silence, I absorbed what I had just learned, let it become what was real in my life. The tension in my muscles finally eased as I accepted this new state of being. My half sister must have felt me relax.

"Fuck him," Felicia said.

"Tried that, but it didn't take."

She snickered. "Sure you gave it your best shot?"

"Not my best *shot* but my complete willingness."

Snickered again. My sister.

"What now?" Felicia said, more soberly.

"He got a telegram, I don't know who it was from. He was banned from San Diego, and that's where he's going. He's taking Peter. He's leaving you." I tried to gather my thoughts, but they were all in a mess. "Eli's got to pay John Seahorse for the car because I don't have enough to do it. He has to . . . " I couldn't think what else Eli had to do.

"Lizbeth, Eli told you you didn't understand him right," Felicia said, her voice uncertain. "And you know you aren't quite yourself, right? After losing the baby?"

"Can you tell me some way that you understand him leaving me now?"

Long silence, while my sister looked at me. She was sad, and she didn't know what to do for me.

"I thought not," I said. "I really hope you'll stay here with me for a while. Or forever. But if not, I'll . . . " I couldn't think how to finish the sentence.

"I'll stay until right before school starts again," Felicia said. She put her arm around my shoulders.

"Do you think he'll tell them? That I have the blood?"

"Have you been holding that inside all this time? Do you really think Eli would do that to you?" Felicia sounded like she thought I was insane. "Listen, I don't like giving blood to the tsar. But if it's what keeps me in school, gives me some standing there, I can go through with it when I'm needed. It's like paying rent for my education and clothes and my boarding. I have a place to be, and I'm safe, and I'm learning how to support myself. Sooner or later they'll find another donor, or Alexei will die, or the doctors will think of a cure. Giving blood is not forever. They can't keep me there if I want to leave, right?"

"I hope I did right by you," I said, and to my dismay I realized I was crying.

"Now I'll do right by you," Felicia said with a sharp nod. She rose and pulled down Eli's travel bag from the top of the wardrobe.

"Come on," she said, and pulled me up. We left the bedroom. Eli was hovering outside, looking; he had no clue what was going on.

"Go on and pack," Felicia told him.

With a helpless look at me, he did.

Peter was in the other bedroom, repacking after only being here a few days. He looked almost as miserable as I felt.

"I don't understand why we're going. I don't understand this at all," he said. "Eli has a plan, but I don't know what it is."

"I am sorry my husband's willing to sell me down the river," I said. "I'm sorry we had a wonderful few months that he doesn't appreciate or even remember, I guess. I'm sorry you have to leave. But you need to go with him wherever he's going."

"You want me to pack your stuff?" Peter looked over my shoulder to ask Felicia.

"No," she said.

Peter flinched. "You're not coming." His voice was hardly audible.

"Not coming," she said. "We'll talk when I get back to school. If I do. If you're in town then."

If ever I saw pain in a face, it was in Peter's. Of the four of us, he was most obvious in his distress.

I was stuck in the moment of numbness you get after a bad wound, and you know in any second it's going to hurt so bad you'll scream . . . but for a second, you can believe it might not be as bad as it looks.

I had had too many wounds to believe that.

For a hot, bright moment, I wanted to kill Eli so I wouldn't have to think about him anymore.

But I didn't believe that would work, either.

CHAPTER ELEVEN

Felicia

I didn't see the explosion coming . . . but I did.

I'd hardly had a chance, with one event after another, to see Eli and my sister in the same room, much less watch them together. I would have sworn they loved each other. Lizbeth was so unlike herself. My sister had always been straightforward, calm, and determined. I had heard that when you were pregnant you could be weepy, though I didn't know much about it. Though Lizbeth wasn't pregnant any longer, maybe her acting so weird was part of the same thing? Eli could not have been more determined not to explain if he'd been paid to be secretive. So either it was a mighty big secret, or he was just being stubborn.

Maybe living in Segundo Mexia hadn't been the great adventure Eli had thought it would be. Or had he found Lizbeth wanting in some way I couldn't imagine? To me, she was . . . not perfect but wonderful. Strong, decisive, hardworking, loyal, deadly, and pretty. Who could beat that?

I was fond of Peter, I really was, but I'd always known I wasn't as focused on him as he was on me. It was a wrench to tell him to leave without me, but it wasn't the agony Lizbeth was going through.

I sat with her on the bench outside while Eli and Peter finished gathering up their things. My arm was around Lizbeth's shoulders. She didn't speak. I could feel her shaking like she had her own tiny earthquake going on inside. I wondered what was happening in her head.

"Screw Eli and the horse he rode in on," I said, and to my surprise, she laughed. Not big, not much more than a choked giggle, but definitely amusement.

"Or the car he wrecked," Lizbeth said. "You sure know a lot of bad words, Felicia."

"Dad was never too careful about what he said around me."

"If I swore when I was little, Grandpa and Grandma would take a switch to me," Lizbeth said. "When Mom was through going to school and started teaching and I was with her, she would just look at me like she was so disappointed. Stopped those words right in their tracks."

Lizbeth had never talked about her childhood. I wanted to hear more, but she fell silent, waiting to hear the door behind her open.

Since we'd given Eli a head start in assembling his stuff, it didn't take long for the brothers to pack. It was just past noon when they stepped out, with bags slung over their shoulders and suitcases.

Eli stopped across from Lizbeth. He waited for her to look up at him. "Lizbeth, I had to leave a box here. Will you send it to Peter? At my mother's house?"

Lizbeth nodded.

Just past noon, they stepped out of the cabin, bags slung over their shoulders. Peter carried his suitcase, too.

Eli stopped across from Lizbeth. "Felicia, can we have a moment?"

I got up and walked away. I needed to talk to Peter, too. I wasn't sure what to say. Word would not help. I hugged him instead. We both cried a little.

"Do you love me?" Peter asked, his voice shaky. "Are you just staying with your sister so she won't be alone? Or are you saying good-bye to me, too?"

This was awful and awkward.

"I'm saying good-bye for now," I told him. I had to be honest . . . but I honestly didn't know how I felt. "You're dear to me, Peter. But I'm only fifteen. I have to . . ." I waved my arm. I didn't know what I had to do, but I had to *do* things.

"When were you going to tell me this?"

I was nonplussed by his tone, which edged on angry. "I don't know what you mean."

"How can you say that?"

I was even more astonished. "Peter, we've been close for a few months, but we're not engaged. We haven't even talked about that."

He wasn't listening. "It's because of the Wizards' Ball next year, isn't it? You want to see what offers you'll get?"

"*What?*" I heard Peter's words, but my brain couldn't comprehend them. Abruptly, I understood.

I'd only learned of the Wizards' Ball a few months earlier. Held every three years, it was a social gathering of magical families. It had become the marriage mart for the supernatural community. Eligible magicians, wizards, witches, sorcerers, and grigoris sent in biographies of their scions of marriageable age, and the families looked these over to make connections that might lead to marriage. This was to prevent inbreeding and continue valuable bloodlines.

I had not thought of it pertaining to me, ever. I wasn't some Cinderella but the child of Mexican slums.

"What about it? Madame Semyonova told me about it. My grandfather met his first wife there. Turns out she was from Felix's family. I don't know what you're talking about." I began to feel just as angry as my sister. "Is this just a day for Savarovs to be assholes?"

Peter looked hard at me. He was not sure I was telling the truth. If he accused me of lying, I would be very angry.

"When we got here, we were happy," Peter said. "How could this be happening?"

"Ask your brother," I said.

"I don't understand any of this." Peter's voice was cracked, and it broke my heart.

I put my hands on both of his cheeks, and I kissed him. "Me either. I don't know why Eli can't be content with his life here, but apparently he can't. My sister can't be alone right now."

Peter gave me a long look, so complicated I couldn't begin to pick it apart. Then he walked over to Eli, and the two of them started down the hill.

I worried for just a minute about how they'd get to the train station in Sweetwater, now that the car was wrecked. But when I saw Lizbeth's face, I threw that worry out the window. Their transportation was their problem. My sister was mine. Lizbeth sat staring into space for a good hour. I was deeply worried. As a rule, even when my sister sat still, her hands were busy. Not today.

I washed the breakfast dishes, put the leftovers in the refrigerator (you didn't waste food when you were brought up poor). Since Lizbeth was still sitting like a sphinx, I changed all the sheets and washed the ones we'd used.

The clean sheets looked so pretty flapping in the breeze on this hot, windy day. They billowed and collapsed like ocean waves. I stood out back to watch them for a good long while. It calmed me.

I wondered if Lizbeth was looking down the hill because she thought Eli would change his mind and march back up to her.

I wondered if it had been the loss of the baby that had triggered this change in Eli. I would have sworn he was a man who'd stick to his promises, and he'd made many of them during the wedding ceremony. Now they were all broken.

I could not keep still. I kept thinking of things that ought to be done. Candle and Jackson should know what had happened. We needed to see if we owed any more on the horse rental—I hated to even *think* of Birdie, because I was as sore as I could be. Even considering how warm it was, a hot, hot bath sounded so good. I wanted to write a letter to someone, anyone, just to relate the events since Peter and I had arrived, but I couldn't think who I'd write to. I was friends with Peter's sisters, but I hardly thought they'd want to hear how I'd let their brothers go. I had some school friends, but it felt odd to think of talking about Peter to them.

When Lizbeth moved, she got up from the bench and went into the cabin. She got the broom and dustpan and swept the floors very thoroughly. She didn't speak, so neither did I. She fried some ham for lunch, which we ate in sandwiches with pickles her mother had put up. They were delicious.

"I reckon you changed the beds," she said.

"Yes." So she had noticed the sheets on the clothesline.

"Was Peter real upset?" Lizbeth said quietly.

"Yeah. He was really unhappy. And a little mad at me."

"I'm sorry about that." Lizbeth looked troubled. "That didn't have to happen."

"Yes, it did," I said. "Else I wouldn't have known Peter was sure we were going to get married, and he could not believe I didn't have the same idea. He immediately accused me of having plans for the Wizards' Ball next year."

"I don't know what that is. Tell me." Lizbeth looked mildly interested. She would talk about anything besides what had just happened.

"Okay." I told my sister everything I knew about the Wizards' Ball: social event, magical people from everywhere. "All the families with an unmarried member between fourteen to thirty-two send in their pictures and biographies ahead of time."

"Then what?" Lizbeth asked.

"All the families look these over to make connections that might lead to marriage. That prevents inbreeding and throws in new talents."

"Like the London season," Lizbeth said unexpectedly. "That was in a book I read. Or also . . . like a stock show."

"Yes, but magical. I hadn't ever imagined I'd be invited. Much less . . ." I was lost in my imagination. The girl from the Mexican slums, dancing and prancing with the magical elite.

"Like Cinderella," Lizbeth said, chiming in on my imaginary pictures. She sounded genuinely happy for me.

"Peter seemed to think I'd be real popular." I looked at Lizbeth, suddenly anxious.

"He's right," Lizbeth said, matter-of-factly. "You're probably fifteen, you come from two magical families, you got Dominguez blood and Rasputin blood, and you're real pretty. If you were rich, you'd be the belle of the ball."

I looked past Lizbeth's shoulder. "Here come your folks."

"Oh, *hell*!" Lizbeth took a deep breath and fixed a smile on her face.

Candle and Jackson had paused to say hello to Chrissie, who had come outside to sew in the bright light. Her whole family had come out with her. Dellford and Rayford were playing with Emily, who was walking from Dellford to Rayford and back again, grinning and proud.

"It's Saturday," Lizbeth said. "Of course. It would be. And school is out now." She sighed heavily. For a moment, she leaned against my shoulder. Then she sat up straight.

Candle was not panting after the climb, but her cheeks were red. Jackson had to catch his breath. They took in Lizbeth's face and posture.

Candle was really pretty, not just "for her age." She had very little gray in her dark hair, and her body was almost as lithe and honed as Lizbeth's. Jackson looked at her with the expression of a man who enjoys what he sees, no matter what the circumstances.

"Lizbeth, Felicia," he said by way of greeting. "Let's go inside, shall we? Candle needs to cool off."

I was a little surprised at this statement, and from Lizbeth's face, so was she. "Of course," she said right away. We all trooped into the cabin. There was a table for four close to the kitchen area, two armchairs and two straight chairs at the fireplace. That was where we sat, with Candle and Jackson naturally taking the armchairs. My sore ass did not like the wooden seat of my chair.

Jackson got Candle a glass of water, though she hadn't asked for one, and sat and watched her drink it all.

This was weird. That had penetrated even to Lizbeth, and she was looking from her stepfather to her mother with her brows drawn together.

"It's good to see you," she said finally, and I didn't think they could tell she was lying. "Is there a special reason you came to visit?"

"We saw Eli and Peter walking through the town today," Candle said. "They were sure laden down. Are they going out on a job? Or camping?"

"They left," Lizbeth said, in a voice as final as a knife blade. "They are gone."

There was a shocked silence.

"I expect you'll tell us more when you feel like it," Jackson said easily.

That was unexpectedly sensitive of him. On behalf of my sister, I appreciated it. I nodded. He nodded back.

"Actually, we came up here because we wanted to talk," Candle said. "This may not be a good time, but I can't wait any longer. We've had a big surprise."

I didn't have a clue.

"What's happened, Mom?" Lizbeth said. "Is something wrong?" She actually looked panicked.

"No," Candle said. "Not really. Mother Nature kind of played a joke on us." She took a deep breath. "I'm going to have a baby."

There was dead silence as we both stared from Candle to Jackson, who was beaming. Hoping. After a second of shaking off the shock, Lizbeth was all over them, managing to sound delighted. I was right behind her, saying all the right things . . . I hoped.

"You're doing okay?" Lizbeth said anxiously.

"Lizbeth, I'm only thirty-six," Candle said. "Of course I'm okay." Her smile was so fixed that I knew she'd been worried herself.

Jackson was also worried but more delighted and proud. This would be his first child.

This could not have happened on a worse day for Lizbeth's feelings. On the other hand, she was forced to think about something besides being left, and that was good. Lizbeth's smile got more and more natural. She asked all the right questions. Candle figured the baby would arrive toward the end of October. She would have to find a substitute teacher for a month or two after that.

"You could quit working," Jackson said, and I could tell it was not the first time he'd suggested it from the pinched look around Candle's mouth.

"We'll work it out," she said calmly. "One way or another."

"Lizbeth says there's not a doctor here," I said. "What about a midwife?" I thought it was strange that Candle hadn't even mentioned Lizbeth's lost baby, but it wasn't the time to bring that up.

"I've been to see a doctor in Fort Worth," Candle said brightly. "I might have the baby there. I'm a bit senior to be a mother again after such a long gap. But there's nothing at all wrong."

We exclaimed and hugged her and made jokes and asked about baby names, all the stuff you're supposed to say.

In Ciudad Juárez, some women had been delighted to have babies, and some women had tried to rid themselves of babies, and some had died in the process of childbirth or child riddance. Those experiences had given me a healthy respect for the process and responsibility of bringing a baby into this world.

Lizbeth rallied amazingly. I was glad to see that Candle and Jackson appeared to be oblivious in their happiness.

After we'd said everything three or four times, they left, hand in hand like kids.

We waved them down the hill and retreated into the cabin, and Lizbeth burst into tears. This seemed to startle her as much as it did me.

"You're happy for them, aren't you?" I said anxiously. "This is okay with you?"

"I'd be a horrible person if it wasn't. I just haven't gotten back to myself after losing my own."

"How did Eli feel about you being pregnant?"

There was a long silence, during which Lizbeth dried her tears and straightened up. "He wasn't . . . delighted. He seemed more worried. Maybe he thought a Savarov shouldn't be born in a place like Segundo Mexia. To a woman like me."

"Did he say that?"

"No, of course not, or he'd have been gone by the time you and Peter got here. It's just something I wondered."

We didn't talk for a few seconds.

I was wondering if I could track down my sister's husband and kill him. But that would be hard on Peter. However, then he'd be Prince Savarov. He might like that? I realized I was thinking of killing people far too easily.

Lizbeth said, "I figure it was about then he began thinking of leaving. Before I might get pregnant again. Before he was stuck here."

"You're making this up, Lizbeth. You don't know that." But that was what I figured, too.

CHAPTER TWELVE

Lizbeth

The worst gunfight I'd ever been in—and that would be the battle at the train station in Ciudad Juárez—did not measure up to the awfulness of the day Eli and Peter left. It lasted forever and was nothing but misery.

At least I had my sister to listen to me and just be there. Couldn't go to my mother, of course.

Everyone in Segundo Mexia had seen Peter and Eli walk out of town with all their belongings. Or at least, they told me so, in every conversation we had in town the day after their departure.

"I guess Eli has an out-of-town job? And his brother was here to help him. That's nice!"

"So you gals are batching it, now that your men have gone camping? Have a good time. Just not too good!"

"I hear Eli wrecked the car. Nothing for us to rent now if we need one. What the hell was he thinking? I'm not surprised he wanted to get out of town. You must have been so mad!"

My mother had held off on telling anyone about her pregnancy and had asked us to keep the event secret for right now. I was relieved, because people giving me their opinions about that would have been hard to take . . . on the same day as people clearly suspected Eli had left me but didn't want to ask me directly.

John Seahorse said I owed him zero, since we'd given him the two extra horses we'd taken from the encampment. Plus, Eli had stopped by to give John enough money to make up the difference and replace the car . . . if John could find one—always the question in Texoma. New cars could be bought in New America, Britannia, or Canada, but they were too dear for Texoma. Here you built a car out of parts of other vehicles that had gone to the great car graveyard. People around here were really proud of using something until it died, in some form or another.

In the week that followed, I also heard a lot of relief (and some mild disappointment) that the militia (everyone agreed that was the right term) didn't show up again.

Then Jackson got a newspaper from the Armadillo area with some shocking news. He let people borrow it after he'd read it. (Felicia and I got it maybe sixth or seventh.) The headline read CAMP OF THE DEAD. The lurid story detailed the writer's horror at coming upon the militia camp outside of Armadillo and seeing "bodies strewn hither and yon with bloody tears dried on their bloated faces."

The horses were all gone, the writer went on to say.

Good. Maybe Standing Still had gotten all of them after he finished with Flowery.

Thomas was listed among the dead in the story, the only local. I didn't hear anyone say what a loss he was.

The writer did comment, with some amazement, that the soldiers' arms lay beside them. "As if they had been felled by a giant scythe."

I called Felicia "Giant Scythe" exactly once. She gave me a look that made me wonder if my lungs would squeeze out air and never let it in again.

I did catch myself brooding over my mistake in leaving all those rifles and handguns. They were valuable, though having that many firearms in my possession would have been highly suspicious if anyone had come looking. I'd only come away with the sentry's rifle. I'd have to wait a while before I tried to sell it.

Felicia read the story after I did. She rolled her eyes as she read a paragraph out loud, one detailing "the horror" expressed by the writer at "the grisly scene of which few people can have ever seen the like."

We had seen worse things than a lot of neat, unbleeding bodies. (Unbleeding except for the tears, that is, and Felicia winced when she read that reference.) "I got a little carried away," she admitted. "Poetic license, my literature teacher would say."

I smiled, which felt funny to my face. We'd been having a pleasant time together. I'd taken Felicia out hunting. We got a deer. I gave Felicia a lesson in butchery, which Dellford and Rayford joined with great interest. (They were quicker to pick up the skill than Felicia.) I sent some deer steaks home with them, before taking some down to my mother. I didn't stay long. I was still having a hard time acting only happy. At moments, I was shocked, tickled, worried, envious, and embarrassed.

Turned out to be our week for free meat when Standing Still brought us a wild pig. He left it on my front doorstep very early in the morning. Felicia got quite a surprise when she opened the door to sweep out the dust. I knew the pig was from Standing Still because it had been killed with an arrow.

After four days of us being alone, Felicia got a telegram. "Arrived SD safely miss you." Peter had signed it.

I hadn't expected to hear from Eli. I was glad that Peter had thought about letting us know. Maybe Eli wasn't even with him. I was simply assuming.

I tried to keep busy, which wasn't too hard. There was always plenty to do. I drew plans to make a crib for my new half brother or sister. I cooked early in the day when it was tolerable, and I cooked outside on the fire almost always. I helped my mother make pickles from her garden. She gave me some green tomatoes, and I showed Felicia how to fry them. I had a quick job escorting the wife of a plantation owner on the leg of her journey through Texoma to Dixie. It was the most boring job I'd ever had. I would swear she wanted someone to try to steal her to make her worth more in her husband's eyes.

No matter how much I tried to ignore it, the loss of my husband was a perpetual dull ache in my chest.

Awful knowledge was scraping away at my heart.

It seemed Eli had not loved me as much as I loved him. He had not been willing to change his life for me forever as I would have for him. He had not shown delight when I was pregnant and grief when I lost our child.

I could not erase or explain any of that, and I didn't see why I should.

I asked Felicia if she was heartbroken about Peter. It was a stupid question, but maybe I wanted company.

She gave me a long look. "I don't think he was my forever," she said. "I felt comfortable with him, happy with his company, but is that the best that it can be?" She looked at me with her mouth all wry. "How are you faring?"

"I miss talking to Eli," I said, relieved to say it. "I miss sex with him. But I must have felt how restless he was getting, whether I let myself admit it inside . . . because I still feel some relief from the tension. And I have to suppose he must not have loved me enough."

When Felicia waited for more, I said, "My pride took a beating. It will recover."

"You'll have a baby half brother or sister," Felicia said. "That should keep you busy."

"Maybe when I get over losing my own," I said. "I never told anyone, for which I'm grateful."

Soon Mom and Jackson would have to let people know, when she'd passed the four-month mark. I could not even begin to imagine the smirks and amazement. I sighed. Yes, I'd build a crib or a chest of drawers for the baby. Something handsome. I'd have to track down a good carpenter to help me. My friend Galilee's son, that's who I'd ask. Or my former friend Dan Brick.

The next Saturday, I was all caught up with chores. Laundry was done, meals were lined up for the day. I wasn't hurting for money, since a couple of people had come to the cabin to pay me for work Eli had done for them. I thought of sending the money to Eli but figured I'd better keep it for a rainy day. If he missed it, he'd let me know.

And I didn't want to think about him any longer.

"Let's go out into the country," I told Felicia. "You can practice." I'd taught her about my guns while we were hunting. My sister liked to learn.

Because I didn't want to have to talk to anyone, we went to the top of the hill and down the other side, rather than through town.

I breathed more freely when we were out of sight. There was nothing but the low hills and the brush, the sky and the birds and the wind. Felicia seemed to enjoy the emptiness, too, which surprised me. She'd grown up in a city, she lived in a city. Now I saw her turn her face up to the sun, her eyes closed, enjoying the moment.

A mile south of my cabin, there was an arroyo. The bank on the southwest side was a gentle slope of about ten feet, but the northeast side was a jagged rock face that rose about fifteen feet, forming a cliff. It was a good place to practice.

This time of year, there was no water running through, though if it rained, we'd have to haul ourselves out in a hurry. No chance of that today. The broad blue sky was nearly cloudless. I'd brought a bag of tin cans, and I set them up on a convenient rock jutting out a little from the dirt slope.

Felicia wondered why I didn't use the rocks on the cliff face for this. "Because I don't want to be hit with a rock chip that makes me bleed or a ricochet that kills one of us," I replied.

When I'd stepped back so far that I was almost standing against the cliff, Felicia shouted "Now!" and I whipped my Colt out with my right hand and fired, right to left. *Ping ping ping ping ping!* The cans flew all over the place. It was very satisfying. I had failed at several things lately, and I felt so grateful to remain good at something.

Felicia laughed, I smiled a little, and she ran over to set up the cans again, or at least what was left of them. This time, when she shouted, I fired left-handed, left to right, and I missed one. I shook my head.

"Four out of five is really good," Felicia called, clapping.

"Unless the fifth one is the one who shoots me back. Okay, your turn."

I reloaded as she shook her hands, like she was waking them up. I set fresh cans on the rock while she did this.

Felicia's grigori training was coming out. She didn't need to use her hands, as grigoris of the Russian school were taught. She didn't really need the traditional grigori vest covered with small pockets, which she would earn when she graduated from the Rasputin School. Felicia did not need pinches of this and that herb, or a set mixture of ingredients, to produce an effect. She had to will it so, and if she was strong enough . . . it was.

When Felicia fired, of course, it was much slower than my work, but she hit three cans, which was very good for a new shooter. She gave me a mocking bow when I clapped.

"Put them back and try again," I called.

My show-off sister willed all the damaged cans back into place, and they glided back onto the rock, settling with an eerie lack of noise. Then, without approaching the sand in the dry streambed of the arroyo, she dug a hole, scoop by scoop. She floated the cans into the hole and covered them up, with only one clank when two of the cans bumped each other. (She frowned at that.) I guessed she was tired of shooting.

I sat on the rim of the sloping side, entertained by my sister's magic . . . until she decided to lift me and move me across the width of the arroyo to the rock wall. But I knew better than to protest when Felicia's skill did not quite match her strong will. I managed to stay silent until the rock wall grew so close I was afraid I'd get my nose broken. I closed my eyes then. After a long moment, I opened them to find my face was about two inches from the rock. I exhaled, hoping I didn't look too surprised and relieved. And I held still. Gently, gently, Felicia lowered me to the ground.

Someone was clapping. It wasn't one of us. I jumped, swiveling to track the sound. There was Felix Drozdov, my brother-in-law, at the top of the cliff. It took a lot of effort not to draw a gun.

Felicia yelled, "Felix!" She seemed absolutely delighted. Felix smiled down at her (almost) as he stepped off the cliff edge and floated down.

Show-off.

"You're unexpected," I said. I meant *You weren't invited*, and I hoped Felix understood that. Probably he did, since he smiled.

"What are you doing here?" Felicia said. "How's Lucy?"

"My wife is flourishing," Felix said. "She has a job."

I couldn't tell if he was being sarcastic or not. Felix had always baffled me.

"Where does Lucy work?"

"At a home for old and ill war heroes," Felix said. "Of course, they are all men." He grimaced. "She is a buffer between the families and the staff, essentially. It's supposed to be the kind of job a woman from a good family can take." He shrugged. "She insisted."

I thought the better of Lucy for working. Hanging around Felix's little house every day while he went out to be a grigori of power? No, not good.

"Why are you here, Felix?" Felicia said.

That was what I wanted to know, too.

Felix didn't seem offended by Felicia's bluntness. He himself had very few social graces, and none of them was natural.

"Why am I here?" He smiled at us, his teeth flashing under his black mustache and neatly trimmed beard.

He was staving off answering.

Even more curious.

"Where are they?" I said, hardly believing he had the gall to ask. "They left. They had to go to San Diego after a heap mysterious telegram. Thought you would know."

Whatever he'd expected me to say, that wasn't it. Felix was nonplussed. He stared at me. "We're all surprising each other today," Felix said finally.

"What do you have to tell us?" Felicia said, tiring of the chitchat.

"Tsarina Caroline has had a daughter, Alexandra Maria."

Felicia and I looked at each other. "Okay," I said slowly. "They're both healthy?" I'd met the tsarina and liked her, but we weren't buddies.

"Yes," Felix said. "God be praised," he added automatically. "And here's the best thing: the son of our tsar is very healthy."

Of course, that was more important, because he was a boy and the heir. I wasn't getting something.

Felicia understood immediately, though. "The boy will not need Rasputin's blood! Girls don't get the bleeding disease!"

Felix nodded.

I had never imagined Felicia had felt she might have to give her blood to the baby boy. And she'd never told me it worried her.

"The only one who will ever need my blood is Tsar Alexei," Felicia said.

"Long may he reign," Felix responded, with as much enthusiasm as if he were telling us it was around noon.

"So my sister's blood . . ." Would not be needed after Alexei passed. And maybe even sooner, if there were other donors. Had Eli's telegram been about this? "How many donors are there besides Felicia?" I said, not even trying to sound casual. Though Grigori Rasputin had been a so-called holy man, he'd scattered his seed in any available furrow. During the attempt to bring down Alexei, several of Rasputin's lineage had been killed, to increase the chance Alexei would die of his bleeding disease.

"We still have the slow-witted boy. And we are on the track of the last bastard's daughter, a woman in her thirties. She has three children."

No one was sure how many generations of dilution would have to pass before the blood was not effective in saving the tsar from his bleeding. Felicia and I were Rasputin's grandchildren. For a holy man, Rasputin had been fond of scattering his seed wherever it might fall, right up to his death at an advanced age.

Now that Grand Duke Alexander, Alexei's uncle, was dead (yes, that was me, too), it was significant that no one had tried to kill Felicia or any others from Rasputin's line. They had been being picked off one by one by Alexander's minions, in the hope that Tsar Alexei would die from his bleeds.

"So he may not need me much longer," Felicia said, as if she'd opened a wonderful gift box.

Felix smiled openly. It looked strange on his face. "That may be so," he said. "So far, the children will not need Rasputin's blood."

"None of that really explains your appearance here in Segundo Mexia. Though it's good to get news," Felicia added. My sister was calm and contained, but I could see she was expecting something exciting. Her eyes were wide and bright, and her fingers were flexing.

"I sent Eli a telegram three days ago. When I didn't hear from him, I came to find him," Felix said, *still* stringing it out.

"Talk, Felix."

I didn't sound anything but a little irritated, but he raised his eyebrows anyway, in that superior look. We'd never been each other's favorite person, since he loved my husband and would never like anyone who held Eli's heart. (Felix could rest easier now, I guessed. I was out of the heart-holding business.)

"All right, all right," he said.

Felicia and I sat in the dust of the arroyo to listen.

"When you defended Tsar Alexei against his enemies at the battle of the Savarov house, he did not forget you, Felicia. He saw you become a warrior. He knew you for more than a blood donor."

We exchanged a look. If Alexei had realized any such thing at the time, we could not remember him acknowledging it. In fact, he had not seemed to recognize Felicia.

Not to say the tsar hadn't done some good and proper things. He had repaired Eli's family's home, which had suffered a lot of damage during the revolution. The tsar had even sent crews to remove the bodies from the lawn.

But after that, Alexei had insisted Eli should leave San Diego, since Eli's stepbrothers and his late father had supported Grand Duke Alexander.

Though Eli had proved himself in the battle, I had fought until I was wounded, Felicia had killed many of the enemy, and Eli's mother had been everything gracious in thanking the tsar for the privilege of sheltering him in her home (despite the broken windows, bullet-perforated walls, bloodstained furniture and carpets, the holes in the lawn which was strewn with bits of corpses, and so on), the tsar had not relented on banishing Eli—though in Alexei's favor, I have to say that most people who had traitorous fathers were put to death or had all their family goods confiscated, and all other family members faced a bleak future.

None of this had happened to Eli. He was still Prince Savarov, though not welcome in San Diego. His mother, Veronika, still had her (repaired) home. Though Lucy and Alice were not tops on anyone's marriageable list, they hadn't been sent to nunneries or anything like that. The two imprisoned half brothers were alive, and so were their families.

"The tsar remembered me? You surprise me, Felix," Felicia said dryly, which was an understatement.

"There, I knew that would please you," Felix said, almost smiling. "Just as it pleases me to hear that you are not so attached to Peter as you were."

"I don't see why you'd give a tinker's damn about who I'm with. I can tell you've got more news," Felicia said. "Spit it out."

Felix, who had no manners at all, made a face. "So crude," he said.

We laughed, and after a moment, he did, too. Well, as close as he ever got.

"You know the Wizards' Ball is being held in San Diego early next year. It's a very expensive honor to host it. Since the Empire is one of the few countries that permit and encourage magic, Alexei and Caroline will attend the opening ceremony long enough to give welcoming remarks and have a dance."

"Then they have to leave?" Felicia said.

I was surprised. In the Holy Russian Empire (which used to be California and Oregon), the rulers were the be-all and end-all.

Felix nodded. "No non-magicals allowed unless they're members of a magical family. But Alexei and Caroline are both curious about the ball. They bade Madame Semyonova to come to the palace to explain it. She has attended the past nineteen balls, in one capacity or another."

Felicia looked awestruck. "I did not know."

"Madame does not talk about it much. It makes her feel old."

"So what did the tsar and tsarina ask Madame?" Felicia said.

"Who from our grigori school was eligible to attend."

"It's up to her?" I said.

Felix nodded again. "In the Holy Russian Empire, it's up to her."

"Who did she pick?" I knew that wasn't a good sentence, but Felix understood. And that was the point Felix had been aiming for with all this talk.

"Your good friends," he said to Felicia. "And you, of course. Also Anna, because she is beautiful and sure to go fast despite her weak magic. Her brother, though he isn't right in the head, for the same reason. A few grigoris who have already graduated. Some of the aristocratic grigoris." And his eyes flicked over to me so I couldn't fail to catch his meaning.

"Dammit," I said. "Eli and Peter." I stared at Felix. "But Eli is married. Only Peter is single. They couldn't have known about this before they left. Right?"

"Might have mentioned it in my telegram," Felix said.

More than one telegram I hadn't known about that Eli had kept secret.

I wanted to kill Felix. And Eli. And just about everyone I'd met from San Diego.

To give Felicia credit, however enormous this news was for her (and the sane part of me knew it was life-changing), she looked stricken when she put her arm around my shoulders. "Felix, you're being an asshole today," Felicia said.

Not just today, I thought.

"The other grigoris attending this ball, they'll have their families with them, right?"

"Of course," Felix said. "The families have to approve the match, so they monitor the process. And sometimes feuds and disagreements get settled at these things, so protection is a good idea."

"Then my family must be with me. And this is my family." She squeezed me to make her point.

"Lizbeth?" Felix sounded like Felicia was proposing to take a monkey to the ball.

"My sister is the best protection I know," she retorted.

"The law in San Diego won't let me carry guns openly," I reminded her.

"We'll find a way."

Felix considered me, his lips drawn up in a sneer. "I think getting her ready will be too much work."

"Lizbeth always rises to the occasion," Felicia said stoutly, and I felt warmed by her good opinion.

And Felix surprised me by agreeing with her. "She does," he admitted. "Now, can I persuade you ladies to give me a place to stay the night? I can start back to San Diego in the morning."

"No, I don't think so," I said. "There's a hotel in Segundo Mexia where you can stay. It's called the Antelope. You can treat Felicia to supper there."

Felicia's brows drew together. She was not happy with me. "You won't come?"

"No. He just wants to talk to you, anyway." I rose, dusted off my jeans, and held out a hand to pull Felicia to her feet. "The hotel's on the square in the middle of town. Can't miss it."

"I'll see you tonight, then," Felix said to my sister.

"See you tonight," she said, though she was not happy. Off we walked. The trip back to the cabin seemed longer and harder than it had been a couple of hours before. Both of us kept our thoughts to ourselves as we climbed the south side of the hill. I was feeling too many things to want to talk. Felicia might have been planning the design of her ball gown. And wondering how to pay for it.

Felicia believed she'd done me a great favor in including me in the festivities. Truly, I'd hoped never to see San Diego again.

If I went to this "ball," I couldn't avoid seeing Eli—maybe his whole family, because his younger sister was unmarried though not magical—at this get-together.

Plus, I'd have to have San Diego clothes. Where would the money come from to purchase them? Last time, I'd borrowed stuff from Veronika. Now she'd probably rather burn her clothes than loan them to me.

Plus, if I'd understood correctly, the dance was in January. By then, my mother would have had her baby, my half brother or sister. My life would have changed again.

I'd thought I felt a heavy weight on my shoulders before. Now I felt like the weight had tripled.

CHAPTER THIRTEEN

Felicia

We were eating a very plain lunch when Lizbeth raised an issue. "Felix likes you," she began. "You're sort of cousins, you told me. And he trained you."

My mouth was full, so I just nodded.

"You think he'll be straight with you?"

"There's nothing Felix loves more than being frank."

"He doesn't like to put ruffles on anything," Lizbeth agreed. "But he doesn't like me at all. Do you think he'll tell me the truth about Eli? Or will he lie out of jealousy?"

"I think he'll tell you the truth if you ask a direct question. Eli may not be here right now, and Eli may have goals that you don't share." That was the nicest way I could think of to put it. "But I *know* Eli would be angry if Felix mistreated or misled you. What dishonors Felix dishonors Lucy."

As if she couldn't help herself, Lizbeth burst out, "I will never understand that marriage. Lucy is smart. She knows Felix doesn't care for women, at least that way. She knows Felix loves Eli. Why did she do it?"

I told Lizbeth something I'd thought I'd never share with anyone. But it would stay in the family. "Lucy doesn't want to have sex. With anyone. Male or female. So since Felix doesn't want to have sex with her, on the surface, it seems like a great solution. He gets a helpmate, she gets out of the house and away from her mother, and she doesn't have to have a man in bed. I have no idea how it's working on any deeper level."

Lizbeth was clearly shocked. "I didn't know there were people like that," she said, not as if she was horrified by the idea but as if it was a strange bit of information. "Huh. Well. Maybe it will be what they want?" She shook her head doubtfully.

"Pretty much what I thought."

"But living with *Felix*." Lizbeth gave an exaggerated shudder.

I laughed. "He's not so bad. He's a good teacher."

Felix walked up to the house with me after dinner at the Antelope, where Jackson kept a close eye on us. But Felix talked about a lot of nothing during the meal and didn't mention seeing any other member of the Savarov family besides his wife. I was surprised when he offered to walk me home. In fact, he insisted on it.

When we reached the cabin, he also insisted on coming in to see my sister. She was not best pleased.

"Lizbeth," Felix began, "you know Eli and I were on the boats together, and also after we landed in California, as it was then."

Obviously surprised at this opening, Lizbeth gave a cautious nod. I couldn't remember if Eli had been born during the long sea cruises of Tsar Nicholas and his family and hangers-on as they searched for a place to take them in. After several refusals, they'd landed in California as guests of William Randolph Hearst, the newspaperman, at the castle he was building in the hills.

"I will tell you something we learned, being in such close quarters for so many years." Felix waited.

Lizbeth nodded, her eyes steady.

"With so many people in such close quarters, it was always best to keep your feelings to yourself. If they were good, if they were bad, you kept them secret. Even from the people close to you, even from family. It was the only way to keep living that way tolerable."

Lizbeth nodded again. She had heard his words.

"Good night, ladies," Felix said, and went back to the Antelope.

"I think he was trying to be nice," I said, when the door had closed behind him.

Lizbeth looked thoughtful. "I think he was, too."

But she didn't comment on what Felix had said. And I didn't, either. We were thinking about his words, though. At least I was. As strange as it felt, I thought Felix had come to deliver that message. And I thought he meant I should not give up hope of Eli.

But then, it was Felix.

After Felix left the next day, I went outside to sit at the picnic table. I stared out over the town into the distance. I felt scrambled, like an egg that had been all whipped up and then scraped into the frying pan.

I was unhappy because Peter was gone. I was having a better time because Peter was gone. I was terrified of going to this ball. I was excited about going to this ball. I wondered how I would pay for proper clothes to wear to all the festivities surrounding the ball. I wondered who would ask me to dance. I wondered how I could learn to dance. I thought of how beautiful my roommate Anna was, and I wondered if she would get a proposal before I did, though I was by far the stronger grigori. Anna's engagement to a rich man's son had fallen through when her father couldn't come up with any dowry for her.

How could I possibly be excited at the idea of meeting many strangers so they could consider my suitability as a marriage partner? It was like being picked at the fish market from a tray of similar fish.

And after I was selected, if I was, I would have to have sex with a man just so I would get pregnant, so my magical strength could be handed down. That wasn't a new prospect for me. The same idea had been proposed because of my Rasputin-inherited blood (since an almost half-witted boy was also a Rasputin grand-bastard). That idea had been disgusting. This idea was . . . not so horrible.

I might as well be appreciated for something I thought was great about me, rather than something that was simply biological, like my blood.

I wondered if Lizbeth was thinking about the same things, but I didn't think so. She had more personal stuff to think of: her lost baby, her arriving half brother or sister, the change to her livelihood that Eli's departure meant, the rejection he had dealt her. And the fact that he'd had so many secrets.

Could Eli really be that shallow? I had liked and trusted him. Now I saw him in a whole different light, but I had doubts.

"Excuse me." There was a man standing across from me who hadn't been there a moment before. Had I been so lost in my own thoughts I hadn't spotted him coming up the hill?

I didn't think so.

"Yes?" I made every effort to appear relaxed. As if she'd been summoned by a buzzer, I felt my sister at my back. I wondered if Lizbeth would question him, but she left this situation up to me.

"You are Felicia Dominguez Karkarova?" the man asked. He was in his midtwenties, brown-haired and brown-eyed, with the narrowest nose and prettiest mouth I'd ever seen on a man.

"I am." I'd never been introduced with my mother's name included. But the time was ripe to do that, because the Dominguez name was really famous. I tilted my head to indicate Lizbeth behind me. "This is my sister, Princess Lizbeth Rose Savarova."

Lizbeth, in her jeans with her gun belt on, looked as little like a princess as I looked like Mexican aristocracy, but we were those things.

"Pleased to meet you both, ladies. I'm Clayton Ashley Dashwood, from Virginia, which is in New Britannia." He inclined his head in a sort of half bow.

The name didn't mean anything to me, though he seemed to think there was at least a chance it would.

"Mr. Dashwood, what brings you to my sister's doorstep?" I asked.

"I represent the Dashwood clan," Clayton said. "We are an old family-based magical group that long ago grew to encompass other individuals of magical ability. 'Long ago' is our problem. We are hoping for an infusion of new talent. Very much hoping." This time, he actually bowed.

I considered this. "Has the power grown weak in your clan?"

"A bit weaker but mostly more . . . erratic. We have retained our considerable wealth and our landholdings, and we have a great deal of political power." Clayton said this not with pride but with the certainty of someone stating facts.

I heard Lizbeth shift behind me. Perhaps she had put her gun back in her holster. Or maybe she had drawn it.

"Did you come this distance to lay eyes on me?" I said.

"It was certainly worth the trip to see two such beautiful women," Clayton said gallantly. "Though I confess I have more than one reason for my journey."

I raised my eyebrows. Pretty I'd give you. Beautiful? No.

"Please do explain. And sit, if you want," Lizbeth said. She herself stayed where she was.

Our visitor smiled and swung himself over the bench opposite me. I should have offered him a drink, but I wasn't the hostess. Plus, this was a business meeting, not a social one.

Lizbeth twitched behind me, and I knew she was thinking of bringing him a glass of water. I shook my head, just a tiny movement, and she stilled.

"I am here to put in my preemptive offer," Clayton Ashley Dashwood said. He was not being boastful. He was serious. "I know there are months until the Wizards' Ball. I know you are a very young woman. But you're extremely powerful and lovely, and you are exactly the new blood we need. I hope you will consider my suit."

"You're not here only as a representative of your clan," Lizbeth said quietly. "You're their best bet."

I couldn't have put it better myself.

"I am the heir and an unattached male," Clayton said, nodding. "I understand money has not built up in your family yet. I am very wealthy."

"So you're sacrificing yourself." I felt a little squeamish but a little excited.

"I would not consider marriage to you a sacrifice but a great opportunity and privilege." Clayton said this seriously and smoothly.

"You're a sweet talker," Lizbeth said. She didn't sound anything but matter-of-fact.

"Thank you. Excuse me, Princess, are you part of the package?"

"I might be."

Clayton took a moment to absorb that. "You are married to Prince Eli Savarov, the grigori?"

"At present."

Neatly put, sister.

"And your talent is . . . ?" Clayton inquired delicately.

"She can shoot the nuts off a fly," I said. I wasn't smiling.

Part of him wanted to laugh, and part of him was a little horrified, and another part was simply interested.

"What intriguing sisters," Clayton said. "I am delighted to have met you. And I hope that my long trip here has convinced you that I am a marriage prospect worth considering." He swung his legs over the bench and stood, leaving us a moment to offer hospitality or to ask him to talk longer.

I didn't do that.

"Thanks for coming," Lizbeth said. She sounded more bored than hospitable.

"I guess we'll meet you again in January," I told him. Now I smiled. "You know my specialty, I guess?"

"I understand you are a very strong grigori," Clayton said cautiously.

"I am. But my most unusual talent is death magic."

My new suitor didn't blanch, but he looked like it was an effort to keep his face still. I had been spoiled by Peter, I saw now. Peter had no problem with me like I was.

"Good-bye, then, ladies," Clayton said, his smile in place. "Until we meet again. Should you want or need to discuss things, here is my card." He produced not one but two calling cards with engraved lettering and placed them on the picnic table.

We both nodded, and then the marriage candidate of the Dashwood clan vanished as suddenly as he'd appeared.

"Neat trick," I said. "I wish I could do that."

We watched the space where he'd vanished for a few seconds. Might he reappear?

"Maybe Clayton Ashley Dashwood would teach you if you married him. I think that he must be the neediest one, to have gone to all this trouble to get your attention," Lizbeth said.

"I bet that's right," I said. "I wonder how many more will come. Will we be woken up in the dead of night?"

"If anyone is in our cabin in the dead of night, that'll be the last thing they do," Lizbeth said, meaning every word.

"Rightly so." If you want someone's favor, sneaking up on them is not a recommendation.

For two weeks after Felix's visit and Clayton's, nothing much happened. I practiced my magic daily, and Lizbeth hunted or shot targets or threw knives (she was also good at that). She taught me some basic knife skills with a Case switchblade. "I took it off a dead man," Lizbeth said. "He didn't need it anymore. Never came out of his pocket."

I didn't ask any questions. I was never likely to carry one of Lizbeth's big fixed-blade knives, the ones she used for gutting and skinning. But this blade, maybe six inches long, would be easy to carry and effective close-up. If I knew how to use it.

That morning, Lizbeth taught me how to hold the knife.

"Now, what will you try to do if someone's coming at you with another knife? Or a club?"

"Stab him in the gut?"

"Can you do that if he's taller, with longer arms? Get that close to him while he's swinging at you?"

As it turned out, I couldn't, even with Lizbeth playing my attacker. She was short and small, but I couldn't get through to her torso.

"So what do I do?" I said, tired of failing.

"What will stop me, for sure?"

I mulled that over. "If you can't hold your weapon!" I said triumphantly.

"Exactly. So how can you fix it so I can't hold my weapon?" In this case, her weapon was an old baseball bat.

"I'd have to cut your arm. The muscles."

"Right!" Lizbeth seemed pleased with my answer, so we reenacted the attack over and over until I successfully did a step inside, turn, and slash that would have disabled her.

"Okay, then," she said when I'd had a chance to catch my breath. "What if you're lying on the ground or in the bed when I appear by you? Can't get my arms then. So what do you do?"

I took a moment to reflect that Lizbeth looked livelier than she had in days. Eyes bright, cheeks flushed, shifting from foot to foot, ready to begin her next attack.

I lay on the dirt outside the cabin, with Dellford and Rayford for an audience. Lizbeth, bat raised, came toward me slowly, giving me time to think.

"Leg," said Dellford in a stage whisper.

I called to Lizbeth, "I should try to slash your leg muscles, so you can't advance." I winked at my adviser.

Lizbeth stopped and nodded, giving Dellford a narrow-eyed look. "You got to let her figure it out for herself," Lizbeth told the boy, who just grinned.

"She would have gotten it, Miss Lizbeth," Rayford said.

Rayford was my champion. He was bouncing his little sister on his bony knee. Chrissie had gone to town and left the boys in charge of the baby, but she'd also parked the grubby trio where we could see them. Now that the boys were out of school for the summer, Chrissie was hard-pressed to get two minutes to herself.

"My mom don't mind having either the boys or the baby, but she can't cope with all three at once, she says," Chrissie had told us that morning. "Mom says she had enough of that when she had me and my brothers and my sister."

After we'd tired of practicing knife technique, Lizbeth decided to show me how to skin a rabbit. Dellford and Rayford laughed till they were almost sick at my attempt. Even the baby laughed. It was way harder than the deer, because the rabbit was so small.

When I told the boys I never saw my food until it came to the table, they were amazed.

"Of course, that's at my school, where I live now," I added. "When I lived in Mexico, I killed chickens." When I could steal one. But I didn't add that.

So I was elbow-deep in blood when my next suitors came up the hill. The man and woman—boy and girl, really—were the fairest people I had ever seen. Their hair was like cornsilk, and their skin was like milk. Lizbeth told me later that I was being overly poetic, but that was what I thought.

We saw them coming, but not in time to clear away the evidence that I was learning how to skin and butcher a small animal. I put down the skinning knife and wiped off my hands on the rag Lizbeth handed me. Lizbeth herself was in a good mood because she was enjoying watching me mutilate the poor critter, and she was delighted when the beautiful twosome appeared.

The girl seemed to be a bit older, perhaps eighteen. She looked at the rabbit for a second, suppressed a smile, and told me that she was Signe and her brother was Skarde.

"We are members of the Helvig family," Skarde said.

Their English was wonderful, and their looks were outstanding.

"Mouthwatering," Lizbeth said under her breath, and then resumed her company voice. "I'm Princess Lizbeth Rose Savarova. This is my half sister, Felicia Dominguez Karkarova. She is the one you have come to see."

"You are vacationing with your half sister?" Signe said politely, looking at me with a lot of curiosity.

"Yes, learning new skills," I said. "Please, have a seat."

As if she couldn't help herself, Lizbeth said, "Can I get you a glass of water?"

Signe and Skarde both declined a drink, but they did sit on the bench opposite ours. Lizbeth had spread out a big piece of oilcloth so I could practice dismembering the rabbit without getting blood all over the table. She wrapped up the four corners and removed the rabbit remains. Dellford and Rayford were having the time of their lives.

"I hunt also," Skarde said. "You are learning to butcher?"

I nodded. "I used to steal chickens," I said. "When I did, my father or my uncle would cut them up to roast them. Lizbeth thinks I need to learn to catch my food in the wild."

"I hope you will never have to do that," Signe said. "But your sister is right, all skills are good to have."

"However, if you chose one of us as your spouse, you would never have to hunt for your own food," Skarde said, sliding that information right into the conversation.

"How come there are two of you?" Lizbeth asked. I was glad she was forthright enough to say it out loud.

"Just in case," Signe said with a sigh. "Perhaps your sister likes women as well, we didn't know."

"What do you think will happen in Norway if the war comes to pass?" Lizbeth asked.

They looked at her with faces that for the first time weren't friendly. "We're doing everything in our power to prevent it," Skarde said. And then they both clamped their mouths shut.

I felt like an idiot. This was obviously something I needed to know about. I'd heard a little here and there. Lizbeth read newspapers when Jackson passed them along. I didn't. But now would not be a good time to ask for background information, since this was the last thing our two gorgeous visitors wanted to discuss, apparently.

"Where are you located in Norway?" I asked, to get into calmer waters.

"We have a large country estate outside of Larvik, in a beech forest," Signe said, much in the way of a tour guide delivering her spiel. "The family spends summers there, and everyone comes, it's wonderful."

"How is it in the winter? I guess the winters are pretty severe in Norway?" I said.

"Yes," Skarde said frankly. "They are. But we go to our city house in the winter, for parties and the holiday and cultural opportunities."

Cultural opportunities. Huh.

All in all, that didn't sound so bad. I'd have to learn the language, I'd have to get used to the cold, and I'd be the only Hispanic person within a few hundred miles, most likely. I couldn't imagine what our children would look like. And if that wasn't a weird idea to be having about someone I'd known for ten minutes, I didn't know what was.

Lizbeth felt compelled to say something since I'd fallen silent. "I guess you all are coming to the Wizards' Ball in January," she said.

They both nodded enthusiastically, and for the first time, they both smiled. It was like the sun came out.

Then they flickered, just for a second. My sister's hand tightened on my shoulder, so I knew she'd seen it, too. Lizbeth's little touch of magic was enough for her to know when it was being used.

It was being used by Signe and Skarde to make themselves more beautiful. Well, fuck it. I was so disappointed.

"What do you really look like?" I said, before I could think. There might have been a strategic advantage to not letting the Helvigs know I could see through their glamor, but my curiosity won out.

Then they were themselves. Still pretty good but not the intoxicating beauty they'd hoped would win me. Their hair was not as blond, their eyes were not as pale a blue, their skin was more variable.

"You're still real good-looking," Lizbeth said. "Why the disguise? You can't keep it up forever."

"We told Grandmother we shouldn't," Signe said. "But she thought if we looked irresistible, we'd have a better chance with Felicia."

In a high, deliberate voice, Skarde said, "First impressions are the most important, and you must woo her and win her very quickly."

It must have been a good imitation, since Signe laughed. But she quickly clapped a hand over her mouth, as if she feared her grandmother was listening.

"I've enjoyed our little visit," I told our visitors. "But I have to be honest, I don't think I'm a good fit for Norway. I would be glad to be your friend."

The two nodded glumly and stood. "Good luck with the rabbit," Skarde said. He gave a little bow, and they started off down the hill. This time, I watched. They vanished at the base.

I had to learn how to do that.

CHAPTER FOURTEEN

Lizbeth

The rabbit was not a pretty thing when Felicia had completed her butchering job, but we could still eat it for lunch. I put it in a pot with some onions and peppers and rice and beer and hung the pot over a low fire. Again, too hot to cook indoors. I'd made some bread early in the morning. The house still smelled of it.

I was just talking to Felicia about what we'd do that afternoon when I noticed a familiar figure toiling up the hill.

"That is my former friend Dan Brick," I told Felicia. "Finally, someone's coming to see *me*."

"Why former?"

"I bet he'll let you know."

I was right. When Dan reached us, he looked at me like I was a roach that had scuttled out of his bathroom.

"Did you do it? Kill all those people?" was his cheery greeting.

"What people?"

Dan looked rough. He needed a shave and some fresh clothes. For the first time, I realized he must have always made an effort for me before. For the first time, I felt a little sad.

"Those soldiers."

"I did not," I said. Felicia had killed most of them. "The soldiers by Armadillo? You know none of them was shot?"

He glared at me.

Felicia said, "Who is this, Lizbeth?"

"Who is *this*?" Dan asked me, not looking in Felicia's direction. As if she weren't really there.

"This is my sister, Felicia," I said.

"Everyone knows you don't have a sister," he snarled. It made his handsome face ugly.

We had been good, close friends for most of our lives. Now that lay in ruins around us. It was sad. It also made me angry.

"'Everyone' can go jump in the lake," I told him. "My half sister, Felicia, had the same father I did."

For a moment, Dan just looked at me blankly, like I was speaking in Hebrew or something. "How did you find her?" he asked, in a voice that was nearly the way he used to talk to me.

"People came looking for her," I said. "They hired me to help find her. I didn't know until then."

"So did you kill them, too?" The sneer was back.

"I married one of them," I said. "Dan, did you climb this hill just to accuse me of killing this person or that person? You've wasted your time, if that's why you're here. If you have another reason, trot it out."

Dan sat down, heavily and uninvited. "I remembered how Thomas always rubbed you the wrong way and what a jerk he was. He tried to friend me up after . . . after you got married. I tried to like him since we were both angry with you . . . but I couldn't stand the guy. When I heard that he was among the dead at the militia camp, I thought about how much you didn't like him right back. Then

Emmie, the kid who lives at the stables? Last night in the Antelope saloon, Emmie told me you'd taken off in search of that Eli and his brother, and they were following the militia. So . . . I wanted to see how you were doing." He finished in a rush.

I don't think Dan had really thought out why he'd come up to see me, but I was kind of touched that he had.

"I'm glad to see you," I said, a little surprised to find out I was telling the truth. "Felicia and I got Eli and Peter away from the militia. Speaking of them, who paid for all that, you think? Hiring those people, getting all the equipment and uniforms? You heard anything?"

Dan's mom and dad knew everyone for two hundred miles around.

"My dad heard—from a friend of his, a guy who travels around selling all kinds of hardware—that an older man who headed this militia group started out in the US Army, a long time ago. He hailed from Albuquerque in New America. He got hired to poke the wasp nest, so to speak."

Felicia looked at me, questions written on her face.

"So you think the militia soldiers were right out of the New America Army, in different uniforms? They were supposed to snatch some grigoris to give them an edge?" In a strange way, that made sense. And it would jibe with what Flowery had told us.

Dan said slowly, "I guess the New Americans didn't want to be blamed for taking a military action in another country. They got a kind of substitute army to do it. Their people but not their people. They needed a grigori to help their war effort. They sent this militia to find one."

"And Thomas Carter had told them just where to find him."

"You know how people talk about anything new around

here," Dan said, smiling just a little. "You get a grigori who works in these parts, people are going to talk. Especially one who's married to a local girl." And the smile vanished. He just looked . . . sad.

I'd been very angry at Dan the last time I'd seen him. But at this minute, it felt good to be talking to him, to see his face, even to see that green-and-brown plaid shirt he should have thrown away years ago. I had to bite the inside of my mouth to keep from blurting out any of those feelings.

"Did I hear right? You getting married?" I said instead.

And we were back in the real world.

"Yeah," Dan said. "MaryAnne Miller."

"I remember her. We went to school together." I hadn't seen MaryAnne in at least three years, but I remembered her as a calm girl, flat-faced, with a deliberate walk and an orderly way about her.

"Her dad's got a grocery warehouse business," Dan said. The Miller place was located about the same distance from seven or eight small towns, all with their own groceries.

"That'll be handy." Dan's family had gone from making bricks in Britannia to making bread here.

"That's what my mom thought," Dan said, lifting one shoulder.

Dan's mom was a strong woman. I'd always liked her.

"And you, what do you think?" I said, treading on dangerous ground.

Dan looked down at his hands. "I think we'll do okay," he said. "She's a good woman, MaryAnne. Got a good head on her shoulders."

MaryAnne had probably never killed anything in her life aside from a chicken for supper or a varmint in the chicken yard. That was a strange thought. It startled me right back to reality.

"I wish you well," I said. "I really do."

Dan took his leave right after that. He'd cycled from angry to sad to resigned.

Felicia said, "If you'd asked him, he'd have shucked off that MaryAnne like yesterday's underwear."

"I know," I said. "But I couldn't do that to him."

"Give him hope?"

I nodded. "Dan needs someone who'll live," I said, working my way through my thoughts. "He needs someone who'll stay home to raise the kids, not go off shooting strangers for a living."

"That didn't bother you when you took on Eli?" Felicia was really trying to understand.

"I just knew Eli and I were meant to be together, and I really believed it. I never thought about our future, or children, or . . . anything, really, except how much I wanted him."

"Do you think you made a mistake?" Felicia sat down where Dan had been and put her hands over mine.

"I don't know," I said. And that was confusing to me, because usually I knew exactly what I needed to do, and I went and did it. "I have been very upset that he had all these ideas and this discontent I never suspected." I still felt like a fool when I thought about it. "What do you think?"

Felicia looked surprised. "You shouldn't even ask me. I'm your sister. I'm always going to be on your side. But since you did ask, I think you and Eli are overdue for a long and honest talk about what you want out of this marriage and if you can find it with each other."

"That's sure to hurt," I said grimly.

"And this doesn't?"

CHAPTER FIFTEEN

Felicia

I was not qualified to give my sister advice on her marriage. I had never gotten to observe a marriage close-up, especially a good one. At least Lizbeth had lived in a happy house (as far as I could tell) after her mother had married Jackson.

Now that I was thinking about them, there was something I had to mention to Lizbeth. "We haven't had a good visit with your mother since she told us about her pregnancy. We need to do that." I couldn't put it any plainer. I didn't know what Candle was expecting from her daughter, but it wasn't silence and drop in/drop out visits.

Lizbeth looked stricken. "You're right," she said. "I've been so wrapped up in my own situation . . ."

She leaped to her feet and disappeared into the cabin. In less than a minute, she came out with a small quilt folded over her arm. It was a baby quilt, and it was faded from having been washed often. It had started out a bright pink and green, I figured.

"Take the rabbit off the fire," she said.

With a cloth wrapped around my hand, I lifted the pot and carried it into the house to leave on the stove, covering it with the same cloth.

Lizbeth started down the hill, and I trailed behind her. Evidently, we were going to make up for our visiting deficiency right now.

The people we passed looked at us curiously. Most of them hadn't met me, and all of them had heard that Eli and Peter had left town. They didn't know what that meant, if we were grieving, if the brothers were on some secret mission . . . they just didn't know. But Lizbeth didn't have time for them. She strode forward, the blanket clutched to her chest.

At the Skidder front door, Lizbeth stopped and knocked in a pattern. One, two, break. One, two.

The door flew open, and there was Lizbeth's mom, flour all over her hands. Her smile was eager and hopeful, and her joy when she saw her daughter was real. She opened her arms and gathered Lizbeth in, flour and all.

I looked off into the distance to give them privacy, but then I found myself in the same embrace. I was startled enough to put my arms around Candle as she'd flung hers around me.

"I'm so glad to see you girls," she said. "Come on in, I'm making chicken and dumplings!"

The Skidder house was large and fancy compared with Lizbeth's cabin. It was built of stone and mortar, and the main room was much larger. Jackson must have been at the Antelope, because I didn't catch a glimpse of him. Candle pointed at the kitchen table, and we took our seats. She resumed her chair at one end, where she'd been making the dumplings. The chicken was already in a pot on the stove.

"Jackson will be home in a while. You two need to stay to lunch," Candle said, smiling as she worked.

We'd made her day, just by showing up.

That was what mothers should be like. I hadn't known what I'd missed out on until that moment. I felt socked in the gut.

"What you got with you?" Candle said, her back to us.

Lizbeth cleared her throat. "I brought my old quilt, the one Grandma made me," she said. "For the new baby."

Candle even had flour on her cheeks. The tears made runnels running down as she worked. "That's mighty thoughtful," she said. "Thanks, honey."

This was obviously very significant to both of them, though I wasn't sure why. I was glad Lizbeth had thought of it. Everything seemed to be okay between her and her mother.

When Jackson came in, he was just as glad to see his stepdaughter as her own mother had been.

I understood for the first time that though my sister had been conceived in the violence of rape, she had been raised in love.

My history? Just the opposite.

As I sat on a stool close to the stove, working all this around in my head, Jackson asked Lizbeth, "Have you heard from your husband? Couple of people asked me, saying they wanted to hire Eli for something. Maybe they were just being nosy."

Lizbeth sighed. "Segundo Mexia is too small for Eli, I guess. It appears he's left me. Maybe I'm too boring for him, since I'm not a grigori."

"That's not what he said at all," I protested. I couldn't remember exactly what Eli *had* said since I hadn't been present for some of the conversation, but Eli was not stupid enough to say those words.

Lizbeth shrugged, just a little lift of her shoulder. "Close enough."

"I thought better of him than that," Candle said. She sat down, her floury hands on her apron.

Jackson looked next door to murderous.

"He would have stayed if the baby had stuck," I said, sounding fierce. I stopped dead as three faces swung toward me, two of them blank and one of them narrow-eyed.

Oh, shit. Lizbeth's mom and stepdad hadn't known she was pregnant. That would have been good information to know. I closed my eyes so I wouldn't have to meet that accusing look.

Candle said, "Oh, honey, you never . . . and then we came to tell you when you must have been feeling . . ."

Her eyes were all bright and wide because she was trying not to cry. Jackson's face was even harder, like it had been carved out of rock.

I wished I could vanish in a puff of smoke. Lizbeth wished that, too. I started to apologize, then realized it was wiser to keep silent and look down at my hands.

"Mom, Jackson," Lizbeth said, very firmly. "Never ever think I'm not happy as I can be that you all are going to have a baby. Someday I'll have one, too. Just not now."

Well done, sister, I thought. Why couldn't I have thought twice and kept my mouth shut?

There was a bubbly sound from the stove, and Candle jumped up to stir the chicken and return to the dumplings. I grabbed a rag and started wiping flour off the table, just to be moving. Candle gave me an abstracted smile. Her thoughts were obviously far away. Jackson was talking to Lizbeth steadily, trying to keep the moment patched together.

Candle whispered, "Did that son of a bitch leave her because she was pregnant?" Her voice was so low I knew Lizbeth hadn't heard.

"Not till after she lost the baby," I said. "If he's left for good at all."

"Then I'll let him live."

Suddenly, I understood a lot more about Lizbeth.

Candle dropped the bits of dough into the chicken broth with a steady, careful hand, stirring with the other. I was right by her, interested in how she managed.

"Do you think he'll come back?" she asked. I was right next to her, and I had trouble hearing her words.

"I have no idea. Lizbeth had to rescue him from a bad situation. I didn't think he was so petty that he would be angry to be saved by her. I also never thought he was so swollen in the head that he would feel he was too good for Segundo Mexia. I think Eli knows something we don't know."

"I hope so. I had a pretty good opinion of him until many, many people told us they'd seen him heading out of town without Lizbeth."

"I like Eli's mother, pretty much," I offered.

"Oh, you know her and the girls?"

"Yes. You know, through Peter. And I was in Lucy's wedding."

Jackson took Lizbeth outside to show her something. A new ax?

"So you're friends of the Savarov family," Candle said.

"Yes, ma'am. Peter and I are pretty close." *Or at least, we had been.*

Candle stirred a pot of green beans. It was really hot in the house. She was flushed. "You don't sound very sure about that."

"He's a good man. I'm not so good."

Candle kept a smile stuck on her face. "But you're honest."

"I am when I can be."

"You look a little bit like your father," she said, out of the blue.

I didn't know what to say. "I hope that's not too awful for you," I offered.

"It was long ago, and it feels even longer now. I was so horrified when I realized I was pregnant then. What he did to me felt like a bad dream." She shook her head, and a strand of hair plastered itself to her damp cheek. "But it got me Lizbeth. And eventually, it got me to this place, with Jackson, who would never raise a hand to me or ask me to do something wrong. And now I'll have a baby I got from love."

I drew in a breath to say something real stupid, but Candle wasn't through.

"It does me good to see you two together," she said. "And if you ever do anything to hurt your sister, if she doesn't correct you, I will." Candle raised her eyes and looked at me directly.

"Yes, ma'am," I said.

I was relieved when Jackson and Lizbeth came back in. We sat down to lunch after Candle had taken the blanket into the room that would be the baby's.

The chicken and dumplings were delicious.

CHAPTER SIXTEEN

Lizbeth

I went from deep sleep to wide awake. I'd been lost in rest, but now I looked around the moonlit room expecting to see something lurking in the corner. I'd heard a sound.

Must have come from outside. The room was empty.

I was out of the bed as silently as I could move, and I grabbed my guns from their place on the bedside table. I crept across the kitchen to my sister's room. We hadn't shut our doors when we'd turned in, thank goodness.

I crouched in the doorway and said, "Felicia," very softly.

"I'm awake," she said, just as softly. "You heard?"

"Yes."

I could see her lying on the bed. She'd pushed away the sheet. She had on a light nightgown. She wasn't moving. "It's right outside the window now," she whispered.

The fact that my sister was in danger, in my house, where she should have been absolutely safe, made me furious.

I could see the outline of a head at the window.

Felicia raised her hand and began the same gesture she'd made at the soldiers' camp.

"No," I said urgently, and I fired at the silhouette.

The Colt made a sound like the crack of lightning, blowing the silence of the night to smithereens as the bullet shattered the window. It woke up everyone on the hill. Within seconds, I could hear yells coming from the scattered homes as people asked who was dead, what was on fire, and where they should go to find out.

My sister and I were out the door as quick as we could scramble, her in her nightgown and me in mine. We were barefoot and tousled and looked exactly like someone had woken us from a sound sleep. We turned left to look at what was outside Felicia's window.

So we could see better, Felicia made a ball of light in her hand. Handy. With its help, we could see a man wearing ancient jeans and a regular short-sleeved shirt. He needed a shave, and he was in his late thirties or thereabouts. He also had a hole in his forehead.

"That's Clement Saddler," I said, astonished.

"Clement who? You know him from where?"

I couldn't see a weapon. Son of a bitch.

Felicia knelt and put a knife in Clement's right hand.

"Left-handed!" I hissed, and she swapped it just in time.

Chrissie's husband, Lee, pounded to a stop just short of me and looked down.

"Damn, that's Clement!" he said. "What the hell?"

To justify the fact that she was kneeling beside a dead man, Felicia felt for a pulse in Clement's wrist. She shook her head solemnly. (No surprise she hadn't found one, with a hole in his head.)

Felicia stood. I put my arm around her. I didn't imagine she needed comfort, but I wanted to tell her a few things. Another man arrived just then, Rex Santino. He lived close to the base of the hill, so he'd made good time. As a result, he was panting like a dog in the sun.

"You two okay? My God, girl, you got a light in your hand!" Rex said. "Who's the dead man? Dang it, that's Clement Saddler!"

Clement Saddler's family, as you might guess, had made saddles and other leather goods for many years. Lots of the people who lived in Texoma had fled to the area from other parts of what used to be the United States, especially if they'd been in some kind of trouble. Texoma had the least law and the most room per person. When Clement got tired of the family business—or his family had told him to go somewhere else—he'd started hiring out as a shooter and general thug. I'd never heard he'd been very successful at shooting, but he was quite a good thug. He'd be the man I'd go to if I wanted someone hurt or killed if I couldn't do it myself.

"He's got a knife," Chrissie's husband said, really surprised.

"Never heard of him using a knife," Rex agreed. "He liked a gun or his fists."

My arm tightened around Felicia's shoulders. The knife had been a mistake. Oh well.

"What happened?" Rex asked, turning to me. "You want us to get the sheriff?"

The nearest law (now that our sheriff had died) was Cal Trujillo in Cactus Flats. Cal would really hate being woken up to come see a dead man.

"It can wait till tomorrow," I said. "Maybe you could drag him a bit away from the house?" As long as I had help, I would take advantage of it.

The two men each grabbed an arm and began to drag the body. The moment they moved him, we could see the revolver that had fallen under his body.

What a relief! Felicia's shoulders relaxed immediately.

Both men exclaimed about the gun. Rex recognized it as the one Clement had won in a poker game the year before.

We were in the clear. Clement Saddler been outside our house with a drawn weapon that for sure belonged to him. I was justified.

"Could have saved my knife," Felicia muttered. I ignored her.

"Can you put him in my old outhouse?" I said, when the talk about the gun had abated.

"Good idea," Rex said. It was only a few feet away.

Animals wouldn't be able to get at the body, but it would be out of sight. The little crowd showed signs of dispersing. After all, it was the dark of night, and they were hardworking people. Their marvel at Felicia's magic light had faded as their want of sleep overtook them.

I thanked everyone for coming and saw them begin on their path home. I said, "Keep the light, Felicia."

"Why?"

"I got to go through his pockets."

It was a quick job. I found a little money, which I put back. I found a slip of paper, which I did not.

I held it directly under my sister's light. It was a diagram of the cabin. It was wrong, I saw almost instantly. Whoever had drawn it had gotten the bedrooms reversed. Clement had intended to kill not Felicia but me. (Or Peter or Eli. Maybe he hadn't known they were gone.)

"I don't know what to think of this," Felicia said. "I'm too tired to make any sense out of it. Let's go to bed."

We made our way inside. The step up seemed almost too steep. Without a word, Felicia turned right and I turned left. We staggered into our bedrooms to fall on our beds.

After that, I didn't know anything until the birds sang in the morning.

I woke sweaty and grimy, my least favorite way to meet the day. I couldn't hear anyone else moving around the cabin, which gave me hope Felicia was still asleep. I could use some alone time. I showered and dressed and toasted some bread, slathering it with butter and jam.

I wrote my sister a note to let her know I was riding over to Cactus Flats to get the sheriff and should be back by midafternoon or earlier. I peeked in to verify Felicia was actually there and asleep—she was—and headed down the hill.

I had expected John Seahorse would still be angry about the wreck of his car. Instead, he laughed and socked me on the shoulder by way of greeting.

"I've heard of a car in Armadillo that may suit me, and I have the cash for it, thanks to Eli," he said.

I wondered if Flowery Bastard had had a car or maybe Joanie Lang.

Almost no one wrote checks in Segundo Mexia, because few people had a bank account. You either bartered or handed over the money.

"We were real surprised we had cash to hand. We won't ever do that again," I said, loud and definite. I didn't want the rumor to spread that Eli and I kept a lot of cash around. If I'd imagined he had that much, I'd have insisted we put it in the tiny local bank or in Jackson's safe.

If I didn't want to be carrying much money, I stowed what I wanted to save in a hole I'd built in the wall of my old room at my mother's.

"What can I do for you today, Lizbeth?" John asked.

"Since the car is paid for and we're square with you, I wondered if I could have Star for today," I said.

"All right, lady, you got yourself a ride," John said. "We'll get Star ready."

In a very short time, I was on my way to Cactus Flats. The first time I'd been hired by Eli and his then-partner, Paulina, we'd gone to Cactus Flats on the same errand, to talk to the sheriff. At the time, Eli hadn't realized who I was or who my father was. It had been a tricky day, trying to tip off Sheriff Cal Trujillo to the situation without stating it outright. I had a few sharp pangs in my heart, remembering that day when I was just getting to know Eli.

I ran into Cal outside Cactus Flats, which at first I thought was a coincidence. His deputy, Maria Hannigan, was riding by his side. I stopped and let them approach me.

"I was just coming to get you," I called. "I got a situation at home."

"We heard," Maria called back.

"Oh?" Someone from Segundo Mexia had run over to Cactus Flats already?

"Jackson called us from the hotel," Cal said.

"You have one at the police station now?" So Jackson and Mother knew about our visitor. My mother would be all worried. Dammit.

"Yep, we do." Cal was proud of that.

"Well, saves me part of the trip," I said. "If I'd have known that, I could have called you myself."

I turned Star to ride back with them. We chatted on the way. Cal's son wanted to go to a college in Dixie because it was cheaper, but Cal was afraid the boy would pick up some ideas there that wouldn't be good ones, especially considering his last name was Trujillo. Maria had had another baby, a girl this time, and Maria's mother had come to live with her and her husband so they could both work.

When it was my turn, I told them about my half sister visiting with her boyfriend. After some deliberation, I said Eli and Peter had heard of a job out of town and gone off to investigate it. That was why Felicia and I had been by ourselves the night before.

They looked surprised, but after they exchanged a glance, they decided not to ask questions.

By the time we got to the cabin, it was just about time for lunch. I was obliged to invite Cal and Maria to share our rabbit stew. We'd been too tired to heat it up the night before.

Felicia was up and dressed in a skirt and blouse, and she had fried green tomatoes to go with the stew.

My mother had given us half a loaf of bread, and we sacrificed that, too.

After we ate, I pointed Cal and Maria up the hill to the outhouse and stayed well back when they opened the door. They didn't flinch. Anyone in law enforcement (or law breaking) had seen worse.

"That's Clement Saddler, all right," Maria said. "We've had him in the jail before. He thought he was a very tough guy."

"Looks like he met someone tougher," the sheriff said, giving me a sidelong look.

"What the hell, Cal! He was peeking in my sister's window in the dead of night," I said, not having to pretend to be indignant. "It's like he was asking to be shot!"

"True enough," Maria said. "I would have done the same as you."

"What I'm wondering," Cal said slowly, "is why Clement was doing something so stupid in the first place. Who paid him? I don't think this was something he'd ever have thought of doing on his own. I mean . . . he knew you, Lizbeth."

I nodded. This was the wonder, for sure. "I would have thought he knew me well enough not to sneak around my place in the dark."

"But he was at your sister's window," Cal added in the same voice, slow and thoughtful.

"Then he sure didn't know Felicia." I decided against telling Cal about the error in Clement's drawing. That would only complicate things.

"Felicia, had you met this man?" Maria was giving Felicia the same look she gave her daughters when she wanted to hear the truth.

"No. I'd never seen him before last night," Felicia said. She sounded calm and sure.

I could see this struck Maria as suspicious. Maria felt Felicia should be shaken by the death of a man who'd been lurking outside her window.

"You've had experience with dead people?" Cal asked, as if he was only mildly curious.

"Oh, yes," Felicia said. "When the tsar was attacked at my brother-in-law's home, I fought with him to repel the invaders."

This was a part of my life I hadn't seen the need to share with the people of Segundo Mexia, but I'd never warned Felicia about it. Not a big thing. Not like my pregnancy.

"You fought with the tsar? Or with Eli?" Maria said.

"Both," Felicia answered, surprised. It was a huge event for us, and for the Holy Russian Empire, but not so much for the people of my town. They might have read about it in one of the Dallas papers, but that would be the extent of their knowledge. "During the insurrection."

Cal and Maria didn't know what to make of that. And I would never find out what they concluded. At that moment, the air behind Felicia seemed to go blurry. Just as I opened my mouth to shout a warning and Felicia began to turn, a hand reached out of the blurriness, and then the arm it was attached to, and then the upper half of a dark-haired man with a stubble of chin hair. He was smiling, and the rest of him seemed about to step out of the foggy oval, when he was attacked so suddenly I shrieked.

In barely a second, the new man was shoved from the blurry air into the dirt at my feet. Another hand shot out, grabbed Felicia by the upper arm, and yanked her away.

"Motherfucker," said Maria Hannigan.

CHAPTER SEVENTEEN

Lizbeth

The stranger struggled to his feet and looked behind him. He looked as stunned as we were.

"Where is my sister?"

I hadn't realized I was screaming until Cal flinched. I jumped past Cal onto the stranger and knocked him to the ground. I sat astride him, my gun drawn and in his face.

"Where is my sister?" I said again, more growling than screaming.

Maria sat down on the bench beside the picnic table as if her knees had folded. But she rallied to say, "Mister, you better talk fast."

The stranger took a deep breath. I could feel his innards rise and fall underneath me. "Señorita, will you let me rise?"

"No," I said. "And I'm married."

"I can speak more easily if I am upright."

"You can use your hands if I'm not pinning them down," I said. Grigoris always thought they needed to use their hands.

"Oh," he said. "That's sensible of you. But I came here with no intention at all of causing harm. I came to offer my services to your sister. If you are Lizbeth Rose?"

"I'm Lizbeth Rose Savarova," I said, trying to figure out why we were having this conversation. "You do understand I would love to have a reason to shoot you? Start talking."

"I'm trying to."

He wriggled beneath me. I sat heavier, trying to will myself to weigh more.

"All right," he said, resigned to the fact that he wasn't going to shift me. "As I said, I came to present my suit to your sister. I suppose that was her, the girl I saw so briefly?"

"Yes. As you appeared and she disappeared."

"I was sent by my family to join the early list of men who hope Felicia Karkarova will choose them for a mate." He didn't look happy about it. "I live in—well, I've lived all over the place."

"I don't care," I said. "Get on with it."

"Right! More facts, less history. As far as I know, your sister was pulled through the door I'd created to get here. It wasn't me who pulled her through. After all"—he made an effort to smile—"I'm here, and she's not, so it couldn't have been me!"

We all three stared at him. None of us knew enough about magic to figure if we should believe him or not. Where the hell was Eli—or even Peter, or even Felix—when I needed him?

I glanced over at Cal. He shrugged. Maria nodded.

"I'm going to let you up."

"Thank God!" he said, and then looked embarrassed. "I mean, you're light as a feather, don't get me wrong, but . . ."

And you won't believe this, but I almost smiled.

"You have asthma," I said, and swung off of him.

When I was standing, I held out a hand to pull him up. He seemed glad to accept the help.

The stranger immediately sank onto one of the benches by the picnic table. He sat and wheezed for a minute or two. We waited. Finally, he was able to breathe normally. And talk.

"I know, I know, I sound like a whistle. Though most people don't recognize the symptoms."

"A boyfriend of mine had it. Long ago," I said.

"Did he die of it?" The stranger looked worried.

"He died of being shot," I said.

"Oh, good! I mean . . . well, sorry again."

When I'd first hugged Tarken, I heard a strange sound in his chest.

"What's that wheeze?" I said. Tarken was not happy about explaining. He called it "weak chest."

A month later, I'd happened to sit by a doctor in an Abilene saloon. I'd learned a lot about Tarken's problem during my conversation with the doc. Tarken did not appreciate that. He'd viewed asthma as an unmanly weakness.

"What's your name?" I said now, as I shifted off of the newcomer. He looked relieved.

"Chin-Hao Costa," the man said, as he sat up.

That explained why I couldn't figure out his looks. He was bronze, and his hair was black and straight. But his eyes were only a little different from mine or Maria's. His face was flat, and he had high cheekbones. Eli's nose would have made two of Chin-Hao's. He had a mustache and a little beard. No tattoos that I could see.

"Korean and Brazilian," he told me.

Probably had to explain every time he introduced himself, except in Brazil. Or Korea? Nope, Brazil, by the way he formed his words.

"Explain why you're here," I said. I tried to sound very reasonable. I holstered my gun.

"Sure. I bet your half sister has already had a few people show up?"

I nodded.

Cal decided he didn't need to know any more about this. "Maria and me'll be taking the body and going back to Cactus Flats," he said. "I'll let you know if we need anything else. I got to get in touch with Clement's family to come get him or at least tell me what to do with him."

"We need to be quick," said Maria grimly. "Cal, maybe we could take him to the funeral home here? Lizbeth, it's called Fedderman's, north of the square?"

I nodded.

Cal brightened. "I don't see why not. His folks are over at Painter, which is the same distance from Cactus Flats as it is from Segundo Mexia."

Between them, the two maneuvered the body onto Cal's horse, and Maria mounted her own to lead the other horse down the hill, with Cal walking behind. They said good-bye to me, only too relieved to see the back of the strangeness. They ignored Chin-Hao Costa.

Now that I was alone with my visitor, I could be a little brisker and franker. "Tell your story," I said. "You need a drink of water or something?"

"Please," Chin-Hao said. He perked up after I brought him the water, and drank a second glass, too. "All right, then. I am not a Russian grigori, of course, but I come from a family that practices magic."

I nodded.

"It's Korean-Brazilian, as you might have figured." Chin-Hao sat up and leaned back against the picnic table. He was wearing a white shirt, dress slacks, and cowboy boots. I had never seen a hide like the boots were made from. "Sorry I'm not wearing my coat and tie," he said, as if he could read my thoughts. "I knew it was going to be hot. Sweat isn't a good look."

I wondered if anyone in Segundo Mexia had a suit.

"You look okay," I told him, because he expected me to say something.

He looked at my jeans, worn pale blue with many washings, and my old blue-and-white checked shirt, and said nothing. He didn't need to. But this clothes discussion was far from my sister's whereabouts.

"So you came here to court my sister, like everyone else. Where the hell is she?"

Chin-Hao held up a finger. "That I do not know," he said.

He still was not serious enough to suit me. "You came here. She left. At the same time. Don't see how that could be a coincidence." I was absolutely fed up with this guy.

"If I were vain, I would say that one of my competitors stole her so that she could not see the wonder that is me and become attached at once," Chin-Hao said. He seemed to believe this. "But I am not vain."

Right.

"So I think the timing was coincidental."

I waited, though I had only a smidge of patience left.

"I think your sister was seized by someone else at the moment I arrived. I don't travel the way grigoris travel. I arrived here by *chuk-jibup*, landfolding."

"I don't give a damn," I said. "I don't care anything about you, unless you can help me find my sister."

"So rude yet so . . . interestingly straightforward."

I thought I might have to kill this man. "Don't test me any further," I said, putting every bit of seriousness I had into my voice.

"How could you bring yourself to kill me?" Chin-Hao said, sweeping his hand to indicate the wonderfulness of himself.

"Let's find out."

Before he could blink, my gun was out and aimed at his head. But I stood back a little—you never knew what magic users could do. And of course, I didn't want to be sprinkled with blood.

"You mean it," he said, sounding as though he couldn't believe I would kill him. Because of the wonderfulness, I guess.

"So much."

"Let's not put that to the test," Chin-Hao said. "As it happens, I think I can help you find your sister. Do you have something of hers?"

I suppressed all my comments about bloodhounds—I'd seen them in action in Dixie—and I fetched Felicia's nightgown from the cabin. To give the magician credit, he did not leer at it. But he did hold it to him in a way I would not have allowed under any other circumstance. He kind of crushed it to his chest with his eyes closed, breathing deeply. And he rocked back and forth a little. Was this for show? Was he really getting information from Felicia's gown?

Chin-Hao's eyes opened. "What a woman," he said. "And yes, I can track her now. Through the time tunnels."

That didn't sound good. "Can I go?" I said, with no idea what I was asking.

"If you hold my hand, yes. Don't let loose, or you will be lost." The magician said this quite seriously. For once, he was not playing some game.

"All right, then, let's go." I holstered my gun and held out my hand.

Chin-Hao seemed, just for a second, surprised. "I don't think any of my sisters would do this for me," he said. He was stalling.

"I don't care about your sisters. I just have one, and I want her back."

"Brace yourself," he said, and his bony bronze hand took mine in a ferocious grip.

I had a moment to realize I hated magic, and then we were gone.

I can't tell you exactly what it was like. I could feel everything blurring past me at a tremendous speed, all colors, so many places, with a bright pink light ahead of us.

I figured that light was my sister, and it got bigger and bigger until we stopped. Our feet hit the ground again—for the first time, I understood we'd been running before, through time and places and what have you. And now we were stock-still, in a green meadow in some other country, and there was Felicia, screaming, standing over the body of a woman. Coming out of a house a few yards away was a man with a brown beard, who flung up his hands to do something magical to Felicia. Without thinking at all, I drew my gun and shot him. I was very off-kilter, so I had to shoot him a second time to bring him down for good.

The bearded man looked absolutely shocked as he folded to the ground.

Chin-Hao looked from me to Felicia, then back again, and he changed before my eyes. The vanity, the casual attitude . . . all gone. For a minute, he looked like a smart man who was rethinking us. I liked it.

Didn't last long.

Felicia was panting, and crying a little, and I ran to her and put one arm around her, the arm that wasn't still holding a gun. "You okay?" I said, looking around in every direction, wired up to an incredible degree, expecting an attack at any moment.

"I don't know. Yes, I'm okay," she said. "I'm not hurt, I'm just . . ."

"Yeah, me too."

"Who is that? Should I kill him?" She pointed at Chin-Hao, who held his hands up in peace and bowed just to be on the safe side.

"That there is Chin-Hao Costa, and he says he arrived to court you just as you got snatched. I'm inclined to believe him, since he brought me here in time to help you out."

"I would have killed the man, too," Felicia said fiercely.

"Of course. You got any idea who these people are? Where we are?"

"No." Felicia stared down at the woman's body for a moment, then she looked around at the green hills and said "No" again.

Chin-Hao came a little closer, paused to see if that was okay, and then asked, "Did she talk to you at all?"

Felicia took a deep, gasping breath and seemed to collect herself. Her shoulders twitched, and I dropped my arm. "I could not understand the language," Felicia said with dignity.

Chin-Hao suppressed a smile, which was smart of him. He said, "I suggest we look inside the house for clues to who did this."

"Are you trying to keep us here so someone else can come take their place?" I all but snarled the words.

Not knowing where we were made me uneasy on a deep level. I had come here by unknown means. I had to rely on those means to return Felicia and me to our proper place and time. If Chin-Hao was a traitor or a liar, we were sunk. I knew my sister had not ever done this swift traveling herself.

For the first time, Chin-Hao's expression was not amused or confident. "No," he said, almost angry. "I swear to you. I only want to know who has tried to steal my potential wife out from under me. So to speak."

"Another one!" Felicia said. She rolled her eyes. "They're not going to answer any questions. Can we go back to Segundo Mexia?"

"You're a death specialist," Chin-Hao said, cocking his head to one side. "Can you not get the answers to a question or two?"

My sister looked at him blankly. Then she looked down at the woman's corpse, thinking hard. She wiggled her fingers as if she were thinking something through and then began to murmur under her breath, which was not her habit at all. I could not understand the words. After a minute of this, during which I kept scanning the green hills around us, waiting for an attack, the woman's body began to stir.

I shuddered and took a step away. I hadn't meant to, and I'd seen this process before, but it was deeply unsettling. I was glad Chin-Hao was not looking in my direction. His eyes were fixed on Felicia with total intensity. I got the feeling he had not ever watched anyone do this, that he had challenged Felicia without any idea she could actually make the dead speak.

The woman, who was red-haired and pale and freckled, tried to talk. Her speech was garbled, and I could not understand the language. Chin-Hao seemed to know what she was saying, though, since he asked the dead woman a question.

And she answered.

My skin crawled. But I was still holding on to myself, not losing myself in the fear. I had enough sense left to notice Felicia had started shaking. She was close to collapse.

"Wind it up, magician," I said, and Chin-Hao hurried to ask one more question after a glance in Felicia's direction.

The woman mumbled an answer. Chin-Hao said, "You can let her go," and Felicia let the woman fall back into death. She staggered and would have fallen if Chin-Hao hadn't supported her on her left, me on her right.

"Now we will return," Chin-Hao said.

So abruptly it made my head swim, we traveled back through the blur, so swiftly, so silently . . . and we were in front of my cabin, and Chrissie was standing six inches away from me with her mouth hanging open. Chin-Hao folded onto the bench as if he'd never left, but he looked absolutely wrung out, and his breathing was rattly. Felicia sank down beside him.

Chrissie squawked.

"Hey, neighbor," I said, trying to sound calm. "That was a surprise! What can I do for you?"

Chrissie turned and walked downhill to her cabin so quickly I could tell she was trying not to run. I was so vexed I almost wept. We'd gotten along so well, all the years I'd lived up here. Now I'd scared Chrissie so thoroughly I didn't know if she'd ever talk to me again.

Nothing to be done about it. She would let me know if she was ever ready to discuss the sudden reappearance of three people out of nowhere. For a second, I wondered what would have happened if I'd come back into the actual space where Chrissie had been standing. Would I have been inside her?

I could not stand there and stare at my feet. I got Chin-Hao and Felicia glasses of water, watched them drink, and went into the cabin.

There were dishes to wash. Got that done. I filled a tub and put some clothes and soap powder inside. I cleaned the gun I'd fired. From time to time, I glanced outside, and Chin-Hao was still there talking to Felicia. Or she was talking to him.

I read part of a book by a woman named Agatha Christie.

Trader Army's wife had told me Agatha Christie was really famous in England. I'd felt good visiting another country through a book, which was *much better than being transported to an unknown landscape with dead people*.

No magic in this book, just a strange man with a mustache who came from Belgium. I kind of knew where that was, but I'd look on one of the world maps in my mother's schoolroom. Close as I'd ever come to Belgium, I figured.

The day dragged on, and still Felicia and Chin-Hao were talking. It was almost suppertime. I should offer them some food, but damned if I would. Uninvited and unwanted guests had to fend for themselves. On the other hand, he had brought us back from wherever we'd been. Ugh.

I stared out one of the windows where I didn't have a view of my sister flirting. I was thinking about what an adjustment it had been when Eli and I began living together. There'd been some moments we each needed some solitude. We'd had no problem taking off in different directions.

Now that Felicia was under siege from so many hopefuls, we had all this company, all wanting to be her one and only. Was I jealous?

I took that idea off the shelf and turned it around in my mind, looking at it. Might be something in that. But I was as good a shot as she was a grigori.

Why had the events of today made me so angry?

Maybe because I was missing Eli? Considering he had left me, that was hard for me to believe. Maybe because I didn't know if he would ever come back. If he would, I wasn't sure I wanted him to.

Being with a man was *hard*. I wondered if my mother ever wanted to hit Jackson in the head. That led me to wonder if the baby would favor my mother or Jackson. I really hoped my mother. Jackson was a great man, but good-looking? Nope.

I fell asleep sitting in a chair and only woke when Felicia came into the house, smiling and full of herself. Also full of fascination with Chin-Hao Costa. He'd described his method of "landfolding" to her, magician to magician. He'd told her about his family's estate in Brazil, which seemed to be a sort of compound in which every individual family had a home. A very nice home. He had managed to impress Felicia with his family's riches.

Felicia kept talking long past the time I felt like listening.

Finally, I'd had it. I was groggy from the nap and the heat, I was hungry, and I was mad. "I need you to go down to the shack by the school and buy us some tacos or hamburgers for supper," I said.

Felicia stared at me, taken by surprise. "Sure," she said slowly.

I gave her some money. "Thanks," I said. "If you don't hurry, he may have closed up."

I waited until she started down the hill before I took a shower and washed my hair. I felt much better after doing this alone.

By the time my sister came back up the hill, I was more myself. There had been too much disturbed sleep, too much shock and surprise, and a hell of a lot too much of startling and frightening my neighbors. I'd always tried to lead a peaceful life at home, to balance the vigilant and dangerous life I led on the job. Mostly, I'd succeeded.

Not today.

We ate our hamburgers at the inside table. They were good, though I had never been sure they were completely made out of cow. The buns were white, the mayonnaise and mustard were not old, and the pickles had a homemade zest to them. The French fries were still warm. I seldom got them, but tonight they tasted good, oily and salty.

Clean and fed, I was *much* happier.

"Chin-Hao scared me going through that quick-travel magic," I said, when enough quiet had passed. "I don't mind watching magic. I don't mind being with magic users. I really hate magic being used on me."

Felicia was calmer now that the excitement of talking to Chin-Hao had faded. I felt a little guilty about that, but my sister needed to come down from the high of talking to someone whose every aim was to interest her. She needed to come back to the world of now. She needed to feel more like my sister and less like a terrifying magic practitioner. I had never been scared of Felicia until today, no matter what she'd done. But today I had been scared.

"I understand," she said. "If you want to know more about where we went . . ."

"I do."

"We were in Ireland."

I thought about using some really bad language, but it didn't seem worth the trouble. I threw my hand up—*all right!*—telling her to finish.

"The girl I killed was an Irish witch, and the man who came running out of the cottage was her brother."

"She kidnapped you for him?"

"He didn't know about it. I was supposed to be a surprise birthday present."

I could feel my lip curl up in disgust. "Anyone who would enjoy that doesn't deserve to have a woman," I said.

Felicia nodded. "I feel the same way."

"Did she think you'd just lie back and take it?"

"I guess so. Seems like he was a real dominating character, brought her up to believe that her talent was less than his, that her place was lower than his."

"What an idiot."

Felicia nodded again. "But she was able and strong enough to grab me by surprise."

That was food for thought. If the girl really had been the lesser talent, it was good I had killed the brother.

"So that's something you ought to learn?" I said.

"If every single person in the magic world is determined to track me down, I better find out how to guard against that."

"Why now?"

"What? What do you mean?" Felicia gave me big eyes.

I gave them right back. "How come, *all of a sudden*, you're getting offers right, left, and sideways? How come now you're here, in Segundo Mexia, they're showing up?"

"I didn't get these visitors at school," she agreed. "Wait. Maybe I did and Madame didn't let them talk to me! I'm not under the school's protection here, so they're taking advantage of that."

"But how did all of them know that?"

We looked at each other for a few seconds. Felicia might have been a little worried. About damn time.

"I guess someone told them where I was. Who, though? The school is closed to all but a few residents for the summer vacation. I'd be one of those residents if you hadn't invited me here. I know the school wall and grounds are protected by spells."

"So you were safe from being . . . hounded like this while you were at school. But not here. And someone told them that. Can you protect this cabin the same way the school is protected?"

Felicia looked doubtful. "I haven't learned enough about protection. Attack is more my style. I wish there were someone here to help me."

"*Now* we miss Eli and Peter," I muttered.

"I miss Peter a lot," Felicia said all of a sudden. "I'm surprised how much I miss him."

"You seemed to be just fine with your foreign friend for a few hours."

"I miss Peter the way you miss your best friend." Felicia looked gloomy. "Not what he would want to hear."

I had missed Dan Brick the same way. I came down off my high horse.

"I wonder where Eli and Peter are and what they're up to," she whispered.

I hadn't even tried to picture that. After the first hundred times.

I told Felicia I was going to read in bed for a while. I tried to make sense of the Belgian detective for about ten minutes before I turned out my light. I lay awake for an hour before I could sleep.

CHAPTER EIGHTEEN

Felicia

After Lizbeth went into her own room and shut the door, I spent fifteen minutes being angry with myself. I had been aware, kind of on the edges of my thoughts, that Lizbeth was suffering.

I'd known she was angry with Eli.

I'd known she loved Eli.

I'd known Eli had left without telling her where he was going.

But I had never believed until this moment that Eli had left my sister for good, so it hadn't occurred to me that Lizbeth really thought that. If I had ever been sure of anything, it was that Eli loved Lizbeth. No matter what he'd said to her, he would be back. And Felix's strange visit had reinforced my belief.

I'd been confident that any day we'd get a telegram or a letter. Or perhaps Eli and Peter would come tramping back up the hill in person. Sure, there'd be some intense discussions, but all would be well again. That was what I'd been convinced would happen.

Also, I thought any man would be stupid to leave my sister! She was loyal and brave and smart, she was pretty, and she could cook and skin animals—and above all that, she was great with firearms. Watching her shoot was a thing of beauty.

Lizbeth made her own living. She was cool in a crisis. She had a fairly even temper. She loved to be clean. Who would walk away from such a woman?

But she was beginning to believe Eli had done just that.

I could admit it wasn't like a loving husband to leave his wife in ignorance of his whereabouts and his plans. Was Eli back at court whispering in the tsar's ear? Maybe Peter would be a candidate at the Wizards' Ball. Of course he would be! And maybe Eli had imagined that getting unshackled from Lizbeth would mean he could choose someone else, too! Lizbeth and I, for all our excellent skills, were not every man's cup of tea.

Maybe someone like my roommate, Anna, would be more to most men's (and some women's) taste. Anna was not a good grigori or even a very good human being. But she was truly beautiful, and she came from an aristocratic (but nearly bankrupt) family. Her family's lack of money would be a hindrance. Beautiful but poor and weak.

Suddenly, I knew where the tip-off about my whereabouts had come from. Anna Feodorovna's family. They would have been trying to move Anna up in the rankings of desirable girls at the Wizards' Ball. I, too, was poor but pretty and very, very powerful. I would be the number one choice. Either Anna had told them where I was going, or they'd read one of my letters to her. Either way, they weren't going to get away without feeling my anger.

Now that I had a target, my mind started to relax.

Before I drifted off to sleep, I spared a second to hope the tsar was well. Every time he bled inside, he needed Rasputin's blood to stop his from flowing. I did not like giving blood to him, because it was mine and I needed it. But this was the way I was paying for my schooling, housing, and food until I was old enough, trained enough, to make my living as a grigori. Then I would leave San Diego.

I wondered if Tsar Alexei would try to stop me.

This new idea didn't stop me from sleeping, but it did make me have bad dreams.

I woke to the sound of rain on the tin roof of my sister's cabin. It was a pleasant way to wake up. It felt like seven o'clock, thereabouts.

I couldn't hear Lizbeth moving around, which was unusual. I got up to go to the bathroom. The door to Lizbeth's room was closed. She wasn't up yet. Well, yesterday had been a big stress and strain.

I went into the bathroom, not admitting to myself that I was beginning to feel afraid. Everything was all right, nothing was wrong. She'd just slept in.

But I couldn't hear her stirring when I came out. I knocked on her door very lightly. I didn't want to startle her. Seemed like a bad idea with my sister being so quick with the gun.

"Lizbeth?" I said. Silence. "Lizbeth?" I said more loudly.

Nothing.

I turned the knob and pushed the door open.

I knew from the moment I saw the way she was lying that my sister was dead. I didn't hesitate.

This was what I had been trained to do. All the birds I had killed and brought back to life, all the turtles, all the rabbits, the dogs, the donkey, the Irish magician's sister the day before.

I knelt by the low bed and took Lizbeth's hand in mine. She was still warm, which was very good. Wounds were easier to fix, but I didn't see one. Illnesses were harder, but she hadn't been sick. I shut down everything but my connection with her. I felt along that connection, inch by inch, like pulling a string through my fingers.

What had killed my sister was magic. That was the hardest of all deaths to raise. Was I ready to fight the skill of someone I didn't know (I *supposed* I didn't know them) for Lizbeth?

Of course I was.

And I would win.

And I would kill the bastard who had done this.

Kill him dead forever.

I traced the magic back to its source. I could tell that the grigori—or sorcerer or witch or whatever he was called—had not been present but had had something of Lizbeth's. A hair, a piece of clothing, a cup she'd drunk from. I could maybe follow that. But I had to hurry. Soon there would be no bringing her back, at least not as someone recognizable as Lizbeth. I caught the magic's thread after casting around, circling her body in my mind. There it was, black as soot!

I followed it. I had done this before but not with a human being and not with an unfamiliar magic practitioner on the other end.

But I could not be afraid, and I would not falter.

Slowly, carefully, I followed the black thread. I needed to be hasty, because it would fade the longer Lizbeth stayed dead. But if I broke it, there was almost no chance of bringing her back.

The thread was twisting and turning, it thrummed fainter and then stronger, but by the time I reached the end of it, I was not surprised to find . . . yes, Chin-Hao. He felt me when I grasped a hold of his thread. His eyes widened in fear. His smiling mouth changed to a grimace of horror when I seized his heart and squeezed. I could let go and let him live, or I could squeeze harder. Chin-Hao was strong and well trained. He was struggling with all his might to rid himself of me. But he was not sorry he'd done this to Lizbeth, and he could not be trusted to repent. As much as I had liked him, maybe because I had liked him, I had to do this.

I squeezed hard, and he died, and the power of his death rippled through me. It was intensely intoxicating, which was the danger of being the kind of grigori I had become.

I hoped there was not another practitioner close by Chin-Hao who had my skills, or the equivalent, one who could in turn trace his death back to me. Quick as I could manage, I dissolved the black thread between me and the dead man. He had been too lazy or had too dim a view of my skill to take the time to secure himself.

Look where that had gotten him.

I took his life force and thrust it into my sister. I had practiced this over and over, because I knew the risks of using your own life force to restore something bigger than a dog.

After a long, long moment, I could hear Lizbeth's heart resume beating. I could feel lifeblood begin to flow through Lizbeth's arteries.

She gasped, and the return of air to her lungs made her eyes fly open. For a moment, they looked dull, but then the vigor flared back into the blue depths, and Lizbeth was alive.

"Holy Mary, Mother of God," she said, to my surprise.

"You got religion?"

"Chrissie says that when something amazing happens," Lizbeth said very slowly. Her voice was creaky. "If I'm not mistaken, I died?"

"You did. But I brought you back."

My sister stared at me, unblinking. "You and Felix have the same kind of magic," she said. "But you look fine. When Felix brought Eli back to life, it wiped him out, though he used me to help. It wiped me out, too. Came close to killing us both."

"Felix never told me about that."

"You seem pretty chipper," Lizbeth said, sounding more like herself. "I'm going to sit up now."

Lizbeth managed it. There was a glass of water on the crude

table by the bed, and she drank it down. She looked healthy, but she was taking some time to reassemble herself.

"Am I ill?" she asked, just suppressing her fear. "Did my heart give way?"

I could not understand her question at first. "Not that I know of," I said. "Oh, because you died? No, Chin-Hao did that. At least, it felt like him when I traced it back. He killed you remotely. Fucking coward."

"Why?"

If I had been her, I'd have wanted to know, too. "Because he could tell we meant a lot to each other, and he didn't want you interfering with his plans to marry me and take me to South America," I said. "That's my best guess."

Lizbeth had to ponder that. "I don't know that I would have interfered," she said finally. "If I was sure it was what you wanted to do, that you knew the truth about him and his folks."

"There must be something he thought we'd find out that would have made him undesirable," I said. "Because he really put himself out to attract me. But he didn't want you to be part of the package."

"He killed me because he wanted to marry you—or own you—and he thought I was in the way," Lizbeth said, struggling to understand.

"Yes."

"Well, to hell with him."

"That's where he is now," I told her with some satisfaction. "Unless he had the company wherever he was of someone with my skill. At the very least, I have put considerable hurt on him."

"You're the best sister I could ever have," Lizbeth told me. "Tell me how you did it. I was worried about you when I saw you raise the Irish girl for a few minutes. But now that it's me, I'm all for resurrection."

"The Irish girl was only meant to be temporary."

I spent a good five minutes describing the different processes to Lizbeth. It was so pleasant to talk to someone who didn't think I was disgusting or terrifying or creepy! My sister thought I was competent.

"So this was your first time killing long-distance," Lizbeth said when I had finished. "And your first time bringing a human back all the way to full life. I was an experiment?" She tried to grin at me, but it turned out strange.

"Well, yes. They wouldn't kill anyone at the school for me to bring back!" I laughed, and she did, too . . . just a little.

"Glad it worked, and I'm also delighted to hear Chin-Hao is not returning," Lizbeth said. "You think his family will come after us?"

I shrugged. "If a man comes courting a death wizard, he has to know that could happen."

"I know men who wouldn't imagine it could happen to *them*," Lizbeth said wryly. "'Oh, sure, she can do that, but she'd never do it to me. I'm so charming and handsome.'"

"Chin-Hao believed that. And he *was* so charming and handsome. I didn't write him off because he lived in South America. And I did wonder what our babies would look like, with our mixture of races and complexions."

"Black hair, for sure," Lizbeth said, and then she laughed. "Not really an issue now, huh?"

I laughed, too, but it rang a little hollow. "No, not now."

There was a knock on the cabin door, and Lizbeth got up to answer it quite naturally. Good. No lingering traces of death. She was almost out of the room when she wheeled around and hugged me with some force. She didn't say a word.

Then she went to answer the door.

CHAPTER NINETEEN

Lizbeth

My mother had been cooking. A few times a year, she and her best friend, Cora, got together to go through the long process of tamale making, having a good old time talking and working together. The results were delicious.

Of course, I asked Mom in, and she commented on how surprised she was to find us in our nightclothes this late in the morning. (It was late in the morning to her since it was eight thirty.) My mother didn't understand people who slept in, just like she didn't understand people who were idle.

I was having some troubles in my head. I wanted to say, *Mom, I died this morning.* I couldn't. It would be so cruel to tell her. But the sentence was echoing in my head.

"We had unexpected visitors yesterday," Felicia explained, when I didn't say anything. "They didn't leave until late."

Which was not as bad by a long shot but not a good thing to tell my mother, either.

Mom expected us to tell her about our visitors, but when Felicia changed the subject, she was smart enough not to insist. "Your husband needs to come back," she said briskly, as if that would never have occurred to me. "I expect soon he'll be here in Segundo Mexia."

"I hope so," I said. But the words came out sounding hopeless.

"You're having company while he's gone?" She gave me the mother glare, the one that says, *You listen up, young lady, and do as I tell you*.

"An uninvited guest, sent on his way as soon as we could manage," Felicia assured her. "It's definitely my fault, the male company."

"Then I saw Maria and Cal taking the body to the funeral home."

"We were coming to tell you all about it when the company arrived," I said.

"Hmmm" was her reply, but it was a sound full of doubt and disbelief. "Well, you know what you need to do."

Now that I'm alive. "No," I said. "What?"

"Send a telegram to Eli's mother's house. Ask if he's there. If you send it to your mother-in-law, she'll answer. Swallow your pride. Even Veronika will answer a wife who's missing her husband."

Since Veronika had railroaded me into having a swift marriage so a Russian Orthodox priest could preside, Mom and Jackson had not been able to attend our wedding. Mom would never forgive that.

I considered the telegram idea. Veronika might be dancing in the street if Eli had left me—for one thing, she'd be Princess Savarova again, instead of me. I think? But I was pretty sure Veronika would let me know if Eli was there, if only to establish her superior claim to him.

"That's a great idea," Felicia said, because I'd been silent too long and Mom's glare was heating up.

"You're right," I said, as quick as I could. "I'll do that tomorrow."

"Telegraph place is open," my mother said, unyielding.

"Today, then," Felicia said, smiling and nodding. "After you leave, we'll get dressed and eat breakfast and walk down to town."

That wasn't pointed, no sirree, Bob.

"Throw on some clothes, and you can walk with me," Mom said, rising. She was wearing her brightest iron-clad smile. "Anita's making biscuits at the Antelope this morning, and I'll treat you to some."

There was nothing to do but pull on some clothes and go with her.

Off we went, the three of us. Though I was looking forward to eating biscuits this morning and Mom's tamales (*since I was alive to eat*), I wasn't happy about the rest of her visit. My mother was in a bull-headed mood today, and she'd check at the Antelope to make sure we'd stopped in.

We all ate Anita's biscuits at the Antelope, along with some ham, and drank coffee. I'd have enjoyed every minute if I hadn't been thinking about my resurrection. I had hoped we'd shuck my mother and get to walk home straight after breakfast, but no. Mom actually walked us to the new telegraph place, right by the post office. She watched us enter before waving at us through the window with an even sweeter smile. When we got in the short line at the window, she walked away briskly.

"Do we really have to send the telegram?" Felicia muttered. There was someone ahead of us in line.

"She'll check." I had no doubt of that. Mom seldom got into bulldozer mode, but when she did, you obeyed. "It's just like the time Dan and I put Jerry Farnsworth's calf in the post office," I muttered.

So I sent a telegram to my mother-in-law in San Diego. The wording was very simple. "Has Eli gotten there yet (stop) Family news for him (stop) Would like to hear (stop)." My mother's pregnancy provided reason enough to contact Eli. I couldn't just ask Veronika where the hell my husband was. Even though I'd *died*.

I had discovered in the progress of the morning, sometime

around the second biscuit, that I'd scraped through layers of anger and sadness when I'd been dead. When I was brought back to life, I'd seen the genuine bottom line.

I wanted Eli to come back. I loved him. That didn't mean I wasn't mad at him, but it meant that I could see forgiving him. After he'd apologized enough. And then we could work out our lives together. If he wanted to.

"Let me know when there's a reply," I told Maggie Taylor. "Please don't let it sit here."

Maggie, a woman in her forties with dark hair and a hawk-like face, had wide golden eyes that didn't blink much. "If a boy comes by, I'll send him up the hill, and you give him a good tip," she said crisply. "I ain't got time to run up and down while I'm in charge of this office, Lizbeth."

That was me told off. I wasn't anyone's favorite today. "Sure, Maggie," I said, trying to sound meek. In Segundo Mexia, I wasn't the shooter dreaded far and wide. I was Jackson Skidder's stepdaughter or the schoolteacher's girl.

Just to make the day perfect, Jackson sat at our table at the Antelope.

"What did you do to get your mother in a tizzy?" he demanded. He wasn't exactly mad, but he wasn't happy, either.

He listened to my explanation with no expression at all. Felicia didn't help. She was clearly cowed by Jackson, and she more or less hid behind me.

I blundered through the story of the man outside Felicia's window, what I'd done about it, the likelihood of other magicians coming to court Felicia. Jackson looked more and more like a bulldog. He started to give me a lecture about upsetting my mother, but I'd had it.

"Listen, Jackson, I didn't make Eli go, and I can't make him come back," I said. "I held the worst of the news away from Mom as long as I could. Then I sent a telegram because she made me. That's all I can think to do. Eli could be anywhere in the world."

From the number of people who'd strolled by while we were having this conversation, this latest development in my personal life would be all over town by tonight, if it wasn't already.

"All right," Jackson said, after waiting to be sure I'd finished. "You just consider the fact that your mother doesn't need any more bad news right now."

"If I can make news good, I'll do it," I said, and if I snapped at him, I can't say that I blamed myself.

Jackson went on his way pretty abruptly, and we went on ours. I didn't want to talk. Felicia understood that.

And then I came face-to-face with Dan Brick again, for the second time in a couple of days.

"I got married," he said without preamble. "MaryAnne's my wife now."

Dan must literally have walked away from my house to his wedding. I started to say something tart, because that was a strange way to act on your wedding day.

But I took another deep breath. I don't want to harp on it, but being dead had changed me. I reminded myself of how I'd hurt Dan by choosing Eli, by not even realizing Dan loved me, and probably in many other ways.

I made myself smile and kiss him on the cheek. "Congratulations," I said, hoping I sounded sincere. "You know I'll never believe anyone is good enough for you."

Dan smiled, and the world reorganized itself into something happier.

Felicia said, "Come on, Lizbeth, we got to be going," for which I blessed her since I had no idea how to end this encounter.

I kind of waved, and Dan made a short motion as if he were going to grab hold of my arm to stop me, and then his hand dropped to his side.

"That wasn't painful or awkward," Felicia said as we walked away. "Not at all. At least you ended that conversation on an honest note."

"I never knew how he felt until I met Eli," I said, which I hadn't realized until now.

"Too bad. He would have suited you in a lot of ways," Felicia told me. "And good-looking in a rough kind of way."

Probably the same kind of rough way that I was good-looking?

We walked home in silence. Chrissie was nowhere to be seen, nor were any of the children. It would take Chrissie a while to come around to trusting me again. She had been spooked by the dead man at my cabin and the strange reappearance of Felicia and me right beside her, and I didn't blame her at all.

There was a very pleasant-looking man sitting in front of the cabin. He had auburn hair and a face full of freckles, with blue eyes that were deep and bright.

"Not today," Felicia called, as if he were a door-to-door brush salesman rather than another suitor.

"But it is not you I have come to see, young lady."

"My bad judgment," Felicia said. "You're here to see my sister?"

He stood and bowed. "If your sister is Lizbeth Rose."

"I am," I said. I returned his bow, which seemed to knock him off his track.

He shifted around for a moment before he got himself together. "I'm Cillian O'Connor, a friend of your husband's," he told me. "The prince has sent me to tell you he's well and that he'll return as soon as he's able."

Felicia and I traded a look of disbelief.

"I don't believe you," I said. "What's his mother's name, if you're such a good friend of his?"

"I haven't ever had the pleasure of meeting Princess Savarova." But this O'Connor guy was worried, I could tell.

"If you do talk to my husband, tell him he can send a damn telegram if he wants me to know something."

We went in and shut the door, and we didn't look out for an hour. He had left by the time Felicia went to the window.

"Do you think he was really sent here by Eli?" she said.

"Not for a second. First off, all Eli's friends are grigoris. That man didn't have a single tattoo. No vest, either. I think Eli would send a telegram or a letter. If by some chance he did send a messenger, I think the last one he'd send is a really cute fellow."

Felicia snickered.

"I can't think why that Cillian O'Connor came here . . . unless he had to lay eyes on us," I said. "You know what? I think he wanted to check on my health." The minute the thought crossed my mind, I was sure that was the truth.

Felicia's face had darkened. "What if it wasn't Chin-Hao? I could be mistaken. Maybe I killed the wrong man."

"No, it was Chin-Hao, you said so," I reminded her. "You said it felt like his magic. Maybe it was whoever drew the diagram for Clement Saddler. They wanted me to die, too."

"Maybe both attempts were by the same person. He knew Chin-Hao had been here and made a good impression. He learned that Clement had not been successful, so he used Chin-Hao. Maybe my suitor wasn't insanely careless. Maybe he was set up."

I liked that idea much better.

"Why?" I said. "Why would someone go to all that trouble? That's a big hard spell, I reckon."

Felicia nodded. "Yes, it takes a lot of energy to cast. It saps you.

But you're paid back afterward." Then she looked as though she could bite off her tongue.

I remembered how drained Felicia had been after she'd killed all the soldiers. But she'd recovered quickly. I just hadn't thought of it after the strain of trying to get Eli and Peter away.

My sister looked anxious. She thought I'd think the worse of her. "Here's the thing. After you're depleted by the death, you get the life force of whatever you've killed. I'd never killed that many people by magic. It took me a half hour before I got the payback from the camp. And when I grabbed Chin-Hao's thread . . . and I killed him . . . I passed his life back into you. Didn't even think about it. So it took me longer to get better."

"So when you kill 'em, you're exhausted, but if you get their lives in return, it bounces you back. You gave me that magician's life."

Felicia just nodded, like passing a life along was nothing.

"Thanks," I said, feeling real awkward.

"Glad to do it," she said, with a shrug.

I got up and moved around the kitchen. Of course, we'd have tamales for lunch. I was going to serve them with fresh cucumbers (gifts from Rex down the hill) and blueberries we'd picked the day before.

While I sliced the cucumbers, I was pondering. From the look on her face, Felicia was, too.

I figured none of our visitors had understood the number of people Felicia could kill at the same time. They'd heard rumors about her power, but they didn't really *know*. I wondered if such a deep vein of power would really be desirable. If they'd seen the dead soldiers with the bloody tears, I figured they might be too afraid to risk marriage. Was that good or bad for Felicia?

"The only reason I can think of is this," Felicia said, all of a sudden, "and it's going to sound vain. But maybe Chin-Hao didn't want to get *rid* of you. Maybe he—or someone else—killed you just so he could find out if I could bring you back."

That thought hit me like a punch to the chest, the kind that stops you breathing. I leaned on the table for support, because I thought I might fall. *My life had been taken to see if my sister could give it back?*

Felicia's eyes were wide and bright with tears. She understood what I was feeling. She was waiting for me to speak.

"You may be right," I said, and I was proud of how reasonable I sounded. "That makes sense." Only if you were a grigori. "Ah— I hate to say this, but I've been thinking . . . if any of them find out about the camp?"

"I might not be number one on everyone's dance card," Felicia agreed, following me perfectly. "And Sunny Boy—Cillian—who was waiting for us, he was sent to check to see if you really had died and if I really had revived you. He still doesn't know. If we'd thought about it while he was here, we could have kept him and gotten some information out of him," Felicia added, sounding only thoughtful.

But we couldn't replay this afternoon.

So instead of torturing an attractive man named Cillian, we had lunch.

CHAPTER TWENTY

Felicia

"What was it like?" I asked Lizbeth after we'd finished eating.

I hadn't had tamales in a couple of years. These were very good. But once I'd thought of the question, I could only wait so long to ask it. The words popped out of my mouth like a cork. Lizbeth had had an abstracted air to her all morning, as if she was listening to something in her head. Normally, my sister was a here-and-now kind of person.

"What?" She seemed genuinely puzzled.

"Being dead."

"Oh." Lizbeth offered me the sliced cucumbers, but I was too full. She shrugged. "I didn't exist for a while, at least as Lizbeth Rose. I was floating in darkness, but I wasn't afraid. It was calm and quiet. Then I came back. All of a sudden, I was rushing from blackness to the sun. The light got brighter and brighter as I flew forward. There was noise instead of silence. I felt things again. The bed underneath me, your hands on me. And then I was back inside my body. By the way, thank you again."

"You're welcome." I couldn't help but smile at Lizbeth. She'd been so matter-of-fact about dying and returning. But I had the oddest feeling she might be screaming inside.

"I know that must have wiped you out." But Lizbeth was looking at me in an odd way, like she wanted me to confirm that.

"Bringing you back? It was well worth it! You've saved my life a few times." Though now that I considered it, I had not been as exhausted as I'd thought I'd be. "I'll bet no one else in Texoma is having this conversation right now," I told Lizbeth, and she laughed, too.

"I hope not," she said sincerely.

While we did the dishes, I was enjoying the peace and the companionship. But Lizbeth had something else on her mind.

"You got a lot of suitors," she said, to open the topic. "Peter's out of the running? He's single and a grigori from a good family. He'll be in the running, too, maybe?"

"Peter is sweet, and he has been very good to me. I'm real fond of him. We've been intimate. But I've said the spell to avoid pregnancy every time. For all I know, he was saying it, too." I hung the dish towel on its rack to dry.

I could tell Lizbeth had questions about that spell that she was putting aside for the moment. "And?" she said.

"If I was bound to Peter, it would lead to his death. I don't want that on me. I can't say what would happen, exactly. I just feel sure that it would."

"So you're too fond of him to be his wife." Lizbeth liked to be clear about things. Her blue eyes were fixed on me with that intent look that made me want to tell the truth.

"Putting it that way makes me not a very nice person." I could feel my lips smiling, in that *but I really am* sort of way. Actually, I knew I *wasn't*. "But I have to see what else is out there. I have an opportunity most poor girls don't get, because what I have to offer is power. Lots of it, raw and not completely trained. I'm half Dominguez and a bit Rasputin, a powerful pedigree. On the other hand, I killed most of my family on that side. So maybe I'm too scary."

I picked up my spoon to eat blueberries. I expected Lizbeth to finally admit that I disgusted her, that she was harboring someone evil, and I could just get myself back to San Diego. But that wasn't what was on my sister's mind.

"I understand," she said. "Peter is not strong enough to be your husband."

I nodded.

"What's your bottom line? What do you want?"

"I want to be safe," I said, with a passion that surprised me. Some things you just don't know until you say them out loud. "I want to have a home of my own. I want to use my power. I don't want it to just be a threat, like 'If you don't act good, Felicia will kill you with a thought.' I want to marry someone I can talk to, and argue with, without him being scared. And I want to not have to steal for food or count every single penny."

Lizbeth nodded. "I felt exactly that same way. I kill people a lot. That's my job. It's what I got. If you try to take what I'm supposed to guard, I shoot to kill."

"It's the power I have," I said. "Like you said, it's what I got. But sometimes I can restore life, as well as take it away."

"If that gets to be widely known, you're going to be swamped. People will come from everywhere to have their family members revived."

"Felix warned me about that. It's better to keep it a secret. People don't think far enough to know that power has to come from somewhere. If I can give life, I have to get that juice from somewhere. And I can do a lot of other things. I can help with earthwork, help with rain, help with a lot of other spells. I'm just . . . a strong grigori. Even if I haven't earned my vest yet."

"All I can do is shoot," Lizbeth said.

"But you're the best at it," I said. "People give you respect."

"And fear," she said. "They fear me, too."

"I don't think the people here in Segundo Mexia do." I smiled.

"Probably not. I'm Candle's daughter. I'm the girl who built her own cabin and was fool enough to turn down Dan Brick in favor of a Russian grigori."

"Dan Brick looked pretty good." I waggled my eyebrows.

Lizbeth smiled. "We never had sex," she said. "I've only been with one woman, then Tarken, then Eli."

"And how is that?" I gave her a sly grin.

Lizbeth's cheeks turned a becoming red. "Really great," she said, and then she did something I hadn't known she could do. She giggled.

It was nice to have that moment to laugh together.

We cleaned up, moving around each other as if we were dancing. Lizbeth said she was going to lie down for a while. She looked exhausted. It's not every day you return from the beyond. She hadn't had a chance to think about what had happened. Or maybe she was thinking too much.

One of her neighbors had left a bag of peas, so I sat in the doorway to shell them.

The view of the flatland below was really pleasant. It was hot but not horrible, since the wind was blowing. It was easier to think about who might have killed my sister without her standing in front of me.

Chin-Hao was still suspect number one. The magic had felt right for him, the black thread had led to him, and most important of all . . . I didn't want to believe I'd killed a man I'd had a fancy for by mistake.

I should go back to San Diego on the next train. I would be

safe from being propositioned once I was on the Rasputin School grounds. Therefore, Lizbeth would be safe. If everyone interested in me had known my whereabouts so soon after I'd arrived in Segundo Mexia, they'd know when I was back at school.

I'd get my ticket tomorrow. I'd made up my mind.

Before a minute had passed, I had another idea that changed my plan.

Part of it was selfish, and part of it was unselfish, and part of it was sheer curiosity.

I would be alone all the way back to San Diego. That would make me vulnerable, way more so than if I had Lizbeth at my side. That was the selfish part.

Likewise, Lizbeth would be at risk if I took off and left her alone, in case any other potential suitors showed up early to plead their cases. That was the unselfish part.

And my final thought was, if our father had begotten two girls six years apart, obviously he'd had plenty of time before, between, and after to beget other children. Did we have brothers or sisters?

And even after that new thought came an old one. Who had killed my father? He'd died close to here, and his brother had fled the scene to return to Ciudad Juárez to take care of me. At least, that's what Uncle had said. (I'd always assumed he'd run because he was scared he'd meet the same fate.)

And just like a bolt of lightning, I knew who had killed our father.

Lizbeth had.

I was glad she slept through till the next morning. That gave me time to get over the shock.

CHAPTER TWENTY-ONE

Lizbeth

Felicia was up before I was. I could hear her moving around the cabin, and I hoped she was making coffee and preparing something for breakfast. I reached across my bed to feel nothing. It was dismaying how quickly I'd gotten used to sharing a bed with Eli, enjoyed reaching over in the morning to find him still asleep or to find his place warm and smelling of him. I sighed. Enough of that silliness.

I scooted into the bathroom and took a very quick shower to freshen myself. Myself was badly in need of freshening. As the hot water ran through my hair, I remembered that yesterday I had died and come back to life, that my husband was gone, that my sister was in danger, and that I was not very safe myself.

After I'd pulled on clean jeans and a sleeveless shirt, I came out to find that there was coffee but not any breakfast. However, from the smell, Felicia had something in the oven.

"Soda bread," she said, without my having to ask.

Fresh bread for breakfast. I could only smile as I poured myself a cup of coffee.

"So," Felicia said. "Was it you who killed Dad?"

I'd been sure she would figure it out sooner rather than later. I nodded. I blew on the hot liquid and took a big sip.

"You shot him? Over at Cactus Flats?"

"Yep. I got a call from a friend there. He told me the man who raped my mother was at Elbows Up. I waited out behind the saloon for him. He was drunk. He came out to piss. I shot him. He knew who I was when he died."

Felicia sat silent for a long time. "I can't blame you," she said. "And he wasn't a very good father to me. Not any kind of father for you."

The words were right, but the voice was wrong. It was empty.

According to things Felicia had let slip from time to time, Oleg Karkarov had been a pretty bad parent: absent, neglectful, sporadic in teaching her. And there'd been women in and out of the shack where they'd lived, as often as he and his brother could persuade them to come. He'd kept her small so she wouldn't be tempted by (or tempt) men and so she could steal food for them and not get caught. But he'd been a flickering constant in her life, and he was Dad.

Jackson had been good to me, in his gruff way, ever since he and my mother had fallen for each other. I'd had the better part of the deal.

"I am sorry you had a hard time when he died," I said, very carefully. "I didn't know he was leaving anyone."

"I understand that," Felicia said, with equal care. "Here's my thought of the day. If he left you and me, he might have left some other children. Maybe we have another sister or a brother. Or two or three."

"I never thought about it," I said, startled. "Do you have a way to track 'em down, if such are alive?"

Felicia shook her head. "I'll think about it. Could be there's someone at the school who knows a spell to help look for kin."

I laughed. "Not everyone would want to be our kin."

"So true. Well, what are we going to do today?"

"You let go of that pretty easily," I said. If I sounded suspicious, well . . . I was.

"I'm not sure how I feel right now," my sister said. "Let some time pass. I'll let you know."

Felicia would, too. That was something I knew for sure.

No one showed up at the cabin, friend or foe. We washed some towels and hung them up to dry. I worked on mending fences with Chrissie, who had to agree it was a hot day.

We still had tamales to eat, so I made a pot of beans to go with them.

Nathan Farmer, from farther west past town, made his way up the hill to ask if Felicia would help him move some dirt on his farm. He'd heard she was a grigori. In my husband's absence, he hoped she might be willing to fill in.

"I'll come with her," I said. "We'll be at your place in an hour, give or take."

"Why'd you delay?" Felicia asked after Nathan had started back.

"I got to ask one of Chrissie's boys to check on the beans from time to time, give 'em a stir and add more water, feed wood into the stove if the fire goes out," I said. "Plus, you don't know Nathan. I think it'll be better if I'm along."

"He grabby?"

"No, he's preachy."

Felicia shuddered. "Can't stand that."

"I figured. That's why I'm coming with you." Also, I didn't want to be left alone with my thoughts.

"Much appreciated," Felicia said. While I talked to Dellford, she changed into my old blouse and pants for work.

"Your friend Nathan didn't set a price," Felicia said as we started on our way.

"We'll have to firm that up before you start work. Otherwise, he'll keep us talking there forever while he tries to get you to take less. You'd agree just to get away from him."

Felicia laughed.

It was easy to feel better this morning when it wasn't so hot yet, after I'd had a good night's sleep. For at least ten minutes, I didn't think about Eli.

Felicia told me funny stories about the other kids at school and did an imitation of the headmistress, a woman Felicia obviously loved. By the time we arrived at Nathan's farm, we were both relaxed and ready to work.

The farmhouse, with a broad front porch and shingle roof, was quiet as we approached. That was no surprise. Nathan's wife had left a year or so ago with another man, and many people said Nathan had never been so happy in his life as he was now. He had Conchita Santos come in to clean and cook twice a week. Conchita was about sixty years old, and she didn't put up with any crap, so they suited each other just fine.

"Nathan," I called. "Me and my sister are here."

No one answered. Felicia and I swapped a look. We stepped apart to create a wider target.

Out of the corner of my eye, I saw movement. Nathan came out of his barn, twenty yards to my left. I almost relaxed. But there was something funny about the way he was walking. Something not natural.

"Watch out!" I called, and Nathan began to stumble in my direction like the noise had drawn him.

As he got closer, I saw that he was white as a sheet underneath his farmer's tan. His eyes were wide and blank. And there was a scythe in his hand. His reach would be much farther.

"Magic!" I yelled, in case Felicia hadn't realized it yet.

This wasn't Nathan. It was something using his body.

Maybe Nathan was still in there. Maybe he could be fixed.

"Back *up*!" my sister called. "I got to stop him!"

So I backed up, but I'd drawn both guns. "I don't want to shoot him," I told Felicia. "If we can get this thing out of him."

"It's not a splinter!" Felicia screamed.

My sister was truly frightened. We were up against something very serious. I had seen bodies being used like this before, almost been killed by one, but I hadn't realized even Felicia would be worried.

"Would it help if I shot him a little bit, and then you could work on him?" I said.

"Let's try that!" she shrieked.

Since Nathan was advancing on me with slow, staggering steps, I planted my feet, took careful aim, and shot him in the leg.

The farmer should have toppled over, but instead he kept coming. He did not seem to feel either the blood flowing out of his leg or the pain.

"Dammit," I said, and shot him in the other leg. Missed, because his legs were skinny. Fired again.

Finally, Nathan hit the dirt. He was bleeding pretty bad, and he was trying to wave the scythe around, but he wasn't speaking, and he wasn't getting up.

Felicia crept up to the farmer with much caution, staying out of reach of the scythe. She looked him over, shook her head. She sent her will to him, not having to say a word. It took a good long moment, but Nathan fainted and released the scythe. I snuck up to him and grabbed it away. It would be better off in the barn, I decided.

Everything in the barn looked fine—neat and orderly. The

horse and the cow had been fed. So had his chickens. His ewe and her lamb were in their pen. I let the chickens out to scratch in the patchy grass. Then I went back to check on Felicia and Nathan.

"He only went after you," my sister said darkly. She dabbed at the first wound with some salve she'd carried in a tiny jar in her pocket. "Can you see if there are bandages in the house?"

I was half afraid I'd find Conchita dead on the floor, but a quick search told me she'd either escaped or hadn't come to work that day. After I'd made sure there wasn't anyone hidden in the house, I began searching for bandages. It didn't take long to find the bag of clean rags and liniment that served Nathan as a first-aid station. There were some safety pins, too.

I carried the whole bag out to where the patient was. The first bullet had passed through one leg, the third had grazed the other, so we didn't need to probe.

We cleaned and bandaged the wounds, pinning the bandages around Nathan's legs. Then we got him to his feet, and Felicia air-lifted him into the house. He groaned the whole way. We laid him on his bed, the only one, and while I looked in the kitchen for some food, Felicia watched him.

I filled a glass with water and made Nathan a ham sandwich. Nathan had an outhouse, so I was glad to see a bucket under the bed. He wouldn't want to walk on those legs any more than he had to, for at least a day and more probably a week. I found an old cane, figured it had been his grandmother's, and put it by the bed, too.

By then, Nathan was stirring a bit. He didn't seem to know who we were or why we were in his house. We got him to eat and drink, and then he fell asleep again.

After an hour, Nathan woke up. Or whatever had been in him wore off. Whatever it was, it was gone. He was panicky at first and hardly seemed to understand what we were saying to him.

"That woman!" he yelled, his eyes open as wide as they could be. "Get her away!"

"She's gone now," Felicia said. "What did she look like?"

"Like nothing I ever seen in my life." His eyes flickered from my sister's face to mine. When he was sure we were not making fun of him, Nathan said, "It was a woman I never seen before. Her eyes were all glittery, and she made some passes with her hands and said some words I'd never heard. I asked her what she was doing on my land, and she smiled, but she kept on doing this magic stuff."

"What did she look like aside from the glittery eyes?" I said.

"She was real pretty. She was Mexican."

That was about all the description Nathan could provide, but it was enough. The farmer fell asleep again, this time more naturally. I looked over his snoring body at my sister.

Felicia and I said in unison, "Isabella."

CHAPTER TWENTY-TWO

Felicia

Here's another reason I'd hated my grandfather. He hadn't helped my mother when she was ill, he wouldn't help me when my father begged for that help, but when he'd learned I was talented (after Lizbeth got me into the Rasputin School), Grandfather had tried to force me into the family. Why was acquiring me so important to the powerful Francisco Dominguez? So important that he'd risked and lost all his children except Isabella?

Here's your answer: I was the only girl of marriageable age his family could present at the upcoming Wizards' Ball.

Aunt Isabella was still of an age when she could have babies, but she was definitely over twenty-eight. Why my aunts hadn't found their matches at previous Wizards' Balls in their younger and more fertile years and my uncle had not taken a wife was a question I hadn't gotten to ask.

Only Isabella had helped my father out when he'd become a widower with a daughter to raise. She had to keep it secret from her father. She'd smuggled money to my father when she'd had it.

I'd only discovered this a few months ago. That left me with a certain debt to pay, since I didn't doubt she'd kept me from starvation a few times. Dad hadn't exactly been a good provider.

But Isabella had her own ax to grind. She might have tried to help us out regardless of any payback, but now that she was in her thirties and the last surviving Dominguez daughter, I had no doubt my aunt would make use of me if she could.

Isabella maybe hoped she could be my sponsor at the Wizards' Ball. She had to know I would never want that. I would want my sister beside me. Maybe Isabella was the one who'd sent the thug to my window. Maybe she'd sent Cillian O'Connor to see if Lizbeth was dead. Maybe Aunt Isabella had spelled the poor Nathan to summon us to the ranch and then hoped he'd kill Lizbeth—or that she'd kill him and be charged with murder.

That was a real string of "maybes."

"Here's what I like most about Peter," I said, and Lizbeth's head jerked. We'd been silent for a while, watching Nathan sleep.

"What?"

"He doesn't seem to want to use me for anything. He doesn't have ambitions where I'm concerned. He doesn't think of me as a breeding wizard."

"That's a great thing," Lizbeth agreed, with a faint smile. "More important than him having no ambition at all? I recall that was a complaint you had against him."

"Maybe that *is* more important," I said.

We left a full glass of water and the rest of the ham sandwich at Nathan's bedside. On our way back through town, we stopped at Conchita Santos's house. We told her that we'd found Nathan shot in his yard, and we'd performed all the first aid we could, but he'd need her to stop by the next day. Conchita, a stubby woman with thick gray hair, seemed concerned about the farmer. She promised to go check on him early the next morning, some clean bandages in hand. We thanked her and took our leave.

"Someone's real anxious to get rid of me," Lizbeth said, as we continued our walk through town.

"If it's Isabella, I guess that means she's got some man lined up for me you'd object to," I said. "Maybe she believes I'm too much of a silly girl to make up my own mind."

"But she's actually met you."

I felt happy after she said that.

But Lizbeth added, "Maybe he's real good-looking, and Isabella thinks you'll forgive everything if a man's got a cute rear end and a handsome face."

"I don't think I've ever looked at a man's rear end," I said, trying not to be a little scandalized. "I thought that was something men did to women. Looking at rears, I mean."

Lizbeth laughed. "Give it a try, sister," she said. "You'll never just look at faces again."

I laughed, too, and we had a good moment, walking through the streets that were darkening with dusk.

We were still giggling when Isabella stepped out onto the road right in front of us.

"Having a good time, girls?" she said.

She had an accent, but her English was good. My aunt was about as tall as Lizbeth—not very—and had the same curly black hair, but there the similarity stopped. Her brown eyes were like mine, her skin browner, her figure curvier by far. Isabella Dominguez was still pretty, though definitely in her thirties. She was certainly a lot more polished than we were, and her face told me she knew that and was glad about it.

"We were a minute ago," Lizbeth said pointedly. Her hands were on her guns.

"My niece needs to have fun with *me*," Isabella said, and hit Lizbeth with all she had.

Lizbeth flew backward as if a shotgun blast had smacked her in the middle. She landed on her back in the street, skidding a few inches.

I don't know if Isabella had imagined I'd hesitate or had supposed I wouldn't hurt her. She found out different. She struggled more than anyone ever had. It was hard to keep hold of her. She was strong. I heard myself growling through my clenched teeth as I tightened my grip around her throat, though my hands didn't touch her.

Isabella began to thrash around frantically. It was all I could do to prevail. I heard someone behind me, running up. I prepared to fight on two fronts.

"I'm helping you," said a male voice. Then a hand gripped my shoulder. After a bad second, I understood this man was feeding me his strength. "Do you intend to kill her?" he asked.

I managed a nod.

"I would think twice," the man said.

"If my sister is dead, this one dies." I would not let go on that one.

"All right, then," he said, and the grip on my shoulder remained. Due to the boost of power he was providing, I was no longer in desperate straits.

"It's for your own good." Isabella managed to squeeze the words out through her constricted throat.

I released my hold on her throat just enough.

"You need to get out of here now," my aunt said. "This place is about to be overrun."

I glanced left to see if my sister had moved. She hadn't. Her eyes were closed. Her gun was right by her hand. Lizbeth not holding a gun was not Lizbeth.

"By whom?" I said, precisely.

"New America, I think. At least, someone operating out of New America."

"The militia group? That was New America?"

She couldn't move her head, but she wheezed, "Yeeeesss."

"And what do you have to do with that?" I gave her neck a harder squeeze.

"Nothing," Isabella ground out.

"Then why are you here? Why did you hurt my sister? Are you the one who killed her in her sleep? Made it feel like Chin-Hao?"

"No, I did not. But I sent the gunman, Saddler."

"Why?"

"I thought you would leave if something happened to your sister."

I wanted to know about the incorrect diagram of the cabin, but the time wasn't now. "Did you ever think about just *asking* me? Did you ever think, 'Maybe if I talk to my niece, she'll see reason and go'?"

When Isabella said nothing, I resumed killing her, but the hand squeezed my should again, and the voice said, "Think twice. She is your kin."

"And she's trying to kill my sister. I like my sister a hell of a lot more."

"You might need two relatives."

"Doesn't feel like it right now."

"Your sister lives."

I glanced left again. Lizbeth had moved. The relief ran over me like a cold bath.

"Isabella, if you try anything else against Lizbeth, I will kill you without hesitation," I said. "Do you believe me?"

Isabella nodded. She could move her head about an inch.

"Whoever's behind me? Will you promise to kill my aunt if she overcomes me?"

"I so promise," he said. "Is that Isabella Dominguez you're holding there?"

"It is. She's my aunt. That is my sister, Lizbeth Rose, on the ground to my left."

"You're not one for delicate women friends."

"Or enemies. No. I am not."

I let go of Isabella little by little. My aunt put her hand to her throat. Lots of drama.

"This is the thanks I get for protecting you," she said in tragic tones.

"I don't think we owe each other a damn thing," I said.

I was keeping my eye on her every move. Unlike me, Isabella did hand gestures, but I believed it was out of habit. I believed she could rely solely on her will to force her magic to work.

"I promise I won't attack you or your sister," Isabella said.

"That's almost good enough." I inhaled sharply. "Okay, Isabella, explain quick."

"I already have. I thought you would leave this horrible town if your sister died. She's the only reason you're here."

"But why not ask me? Surely that would be easier and more natural than killing my kin?"

"I may have made a mistake there," she conceded. "I didn't want you to know I was involved."

"Why is that?"

"Because . . ." And here my aunt seemed to be struggling to come up with a reason. "You love your sister."

"Man behind me. Check on Lizbeth?"

"Of course." The hand left my shoulder. I kind of missed it.

I didn't dare take a moment to look left again. Isabella had been bested. She would not take that lightly. She would hate it, in fact. She would hate me.

I hadn't been sure I could do it, so I was really pleased. I couldn't let that dull my reaction.

"Your sister is coming to," the man said.

I didn't dare look.

"I promise I won't attack you or your sister," Isabella said again, seeing my predicament.

I didn't trust my aunt, despite her promise. But I had to check on Lizbeth.

As soon as I'd turned, I *felt* Isabella move. I whipped back in time to freeze her in place. Maybe she'd needed to scratch her rear or toss her hair, but any movement on my aunt's part was suspect. I was tossing around my power recklessly, and I was feeling it, but it had to be done.

Now that I'd got her fixed for a while, I was able to tend to Lizbeth.

"Her pulse is strong," the man said.

I couldn't seem to see his face clearly, which would have really worried me if I hadn't been so worried about my sister. His voice made me calmer. I didn't know if that was his magic, or just his natural character.

I knelt to take Lizbeth's other hand. He was right about her pulse, but her hand was limp and cool. Though I knew she was alive, I sent life into her. I was beginning to feel the benefit of all the deaths around me. It was unpleasantly easy. I'd done this over and over under Felix's tutelage, starting with mice and working my way up to birds and cats and dogs and pigs and a horse, draining life and restoring it. Lizbeth wasn't dead, but she wasn't responding, either.

The man did not comment, but I knew he was watching me closely.

I heard Lizbeth sigh. I felt her fingers move in mine.

I felt the warmth of her hand.

"Not *again*," Lizbeth mumbled.

"Yes, again, thanks to Isabella," I said. "She denies killing you as you slept, by the way. But she admits sending Clement Saddler."

"Why?"

"She says she wanted me to leave Segundo Mexia, because it's about to be invaded."

"Oh. If I died, you'd leave?"

"That's what she thought. And she's right, I would have."

"And who are you?" Lizbeth pulled her hands away from the man and me, struggled to sit up. She was looking at the man. "What's the purpose of your disguise? Are there people here who know you, or do you not want us to recognize you?"

"I was wondering the same thing," I said.

"Ladies, I must take my leave," he said. He got up easily and vanished into the darkness.

"Huh," Lizbeth said. "Not suspicious at all."

"He really did help," I said. "With Isabella."

I took her hands to help her sit up. Now that the stranger wasn't around, she didn't mind accepting my help.

"What's happening with Isabella?" she said.

"I froze her. Let's see."

We got up together with a bit of a struggle and made our way over to my aunt. She was glaring up at me.

I propped Lizbeth up against the window of the dry goods store while I let Isabella speak.

"You need to get out right now! They'll be here any minute!" she said, her voice harsh and desperate.

All right, she had me worried now. I let her completely loose, and I put my arm around Lizbeth. We three began to walk together, my sister struggling to make her legs work well, my aunt sputtering with some really bad language and some home truths about my character.

I had caught her sense of urgency. We worked our way up to a good shamble, but that was all we could manage.

"All you had to do," I panted, "was say, 'Hurry, danger!'"

Isabella didn't waste her breath. She gave me a pointed look, and we staggered onward.

"We're trying to make it to the cabin?" I said. I'd realized I didn't know where we were going.

"Her folks', it's shorter," Isabella said.

"No!" The word popped out of Lizbeth.

I understood right away. Her mother was pregnant, and we shouldn't draw conflict that way.

"Antelope," Lizbeth said.

Isabella had opened her mouth to tell us we weren't going hunting, but I nipped in before she could make things worse. "The hotel," I said. "There's at least a shotgun there."

Lizbeth nodded. So we turned around and hastened just as desperately back the way we'd come.

In no time at all, we were across the square at the Antelope. It was still open. Since it was the only nice bar in town, that made sense. It also made sense that Jackson had left his manager in charge, a man from the Hill Country.

There were only five patrons, four of them men, when we lurched through the double doors. The reception desk was right inside the door. The bar and tables were to our right, the stairs to the guest rooms to the left.

"What the hell!" the blond man behind the bar said, more in a tone of wonder. He was very large and had been through a lot of trouble. Scars went here and there across his face and arms.

"Trouble coming," I said. "Go home and arm yourselves!"

I learned to like Segundo Mexia in that moment. In less than two minutes, the bar was empty except for Mr. Tall, Blond, and Scarred.

"Who are you?" he asked, which was reasonable. He was already hauling out the shotgun and checking it over. "What happened to Lizbeth?"

"I'm her sister, Felicia," I said. "This is Isabella from Mexico. She's had advance warning of an attack tonight."

"I know her, she's staying here," the man said.

"I checked in today," Isabella said. "This is Horst, didn't get his last name."

"Wildermann," Horst said, as if that were significant.

Lizbeth made a noise, as if she were trying to tell us something but her throat wasn't cooperating.

"What is it, Lizbeth?" I bent down to hear her better.

"Leave me with Horst," she said weakly. "I will be fine."

Surprisingly, Horst smiled, which made his scarred face wrinkle in an interesting way. He laid the shotgun on the bar and proceeded to drag out a machete and a bowie knife. Then a pistol, brand unknown.

"Up to my room," Isabella told me. "I've got a balcony. We'll have a better view."

I ran up the stairs after my aunt. I was reluctant to leave Lizbeth, but I couldn't get her up the stairs. I knew from previous fights that being above the enemy was a real advantage. Lizbeth had seemed comfortable with Horst. She must have known him for years.

Isabella unlocked a room to her right, and we hurried in. Her room held a long window that opened onto a small balcony right above the main entrance to the Antelope. As I stepped out behind her, the lights over the Antelope porch went out. Had Horst thought that would be a good idea?

There were not too many other lights on around the square. One set winked out as we watched, perhaps turned off by one of the people who'd been in the bar. There was no sound. There was no movement.

Then I caught a flicker to my right.

CHAPTER TWENTY-THREE

Lizbeth

Horst crouched by me in the darkness. He'd come out from behind the heavy oak bar. Just a bit of light was coming through the clear panes in the double doors. The curtains on the window had been drawn.

"Are you hurt? How bad is it?" Horst asked.

He had a trace of an accent; Jackson had told me it was German. The barman's folks had immigrated to the Hill Country south of us when Horst was a kid, and most of the inhabitants of his community spoke German as well as English.

"I'm getting better by the minute," I said. "Isabella hit me with magic."

"I'll rip her from stem to stern," Horst growled.

"Let's take care of our other enemies first. For now, Isabella's on our side."

"And Felicia? That's your half sister Jackson told me about?"

I nodded. I was feeling better by the minute. "Help me up," I said. "I can prop my elbows on the bar."

Horst put an arm around me, braced his other hand on my ribs, and I was standing. We shuffled around the bar so I could situate myself behind it. I put both my guns on its surface, ready to use. Horst picked up the shotgun.

I heard footsteps above us. "They're coming," Isabella called down the stairway, and then dashed back inside her room. I could hear her and Felicia moving around over our heads.

"Shouting," Horst said. "Pretty close."

I summoned every bit of strength I could scrape together. I might die in the next few minutes, but it wouldn't be anything I hadn't done before.

"Easy death," I said to Horst. I'd known him for ten years, at least, and I'd always gotten along fine with him. There were worse people to die with.

"An easy death to you," Horst returned. "But if I can help it, we ain't gonna die tonight."

I almost told him I already had, but I didn't think that would add to his confidence. I'd never gone into a fight feeling as weak as I did now. I'd still do my best. I wasn't going to die lying on the floor or in a sickbed.

One of the voices got closer, and it caught at me.

"Don't shoot," it was saying. "Lizbeth, don't shoot!"

"Why does he think we'll listen?" Horst said.

"It's my husband!" I grabbed Horst's arm. "It's Eli!"

"Oh. All right." Horst didn't put down the shotgun, of course, but he took his finger off the trigger.

My hands were trembling all of a sudden. I lowered my guns to the surface of the bar. The door burst open, and I had a second to think what a fool I'd feel if it wasn't Eli.

But it *was* Eli, and Peter was right behind him. Then they were in the bar, slamming shut the doors behind them. Eli reached for the big plank used to bar the door at night, and he laid it in its slots as if it weighed nothing.

"Hit the floor!" he yelled, and we did, just in time.

Bullets shattered the glass in the door. Horst rose to his feet and aimed the shotgun, but he wisely waited until our attackers were visible in the place where the glass used to be before he fired.

Then there was the usual screaming and moaning. I was ready with my Colts while Horst reloaded. I felt a lot livelier now that Eli was near. I wished I could spare a moment to hug him, and feel his arms around me, and smell his familiar smell. But that would have to wait.

There were men thudding against the barred door now. I began shooting.

In one brief pause, I realized I could hear shooting all over Segundo Mexia: the bark of small arms, the louder sound of rifles, and the boom of shotguns. My little town was putting up a very big fight.

I was picking my shots carefully, since I hadn't brought extra bullets. I had set out that morning with seven in the magazine, one in the chamber of each Colt 1911. I'd used three shots at Nathan's farm. I had to make each bullet count, best I could. After we'd cleared away the crowd around the doors, I stepped out from behind the bar and crept closer. There were bodies piled up on the porch outside. Some of them were groaning, but as long as they stayed down, I was content.

Then Horst got wounded in the right shoulder from someone off to the left side, out of my sight. Horst couldn't hold the shotgun. He grabbed up the machete in his good hand.

I hadn't heard anything from Eli and Peter, who were crouched among the bar tables to my left. That meant bad news, but I couldn't spare a second to ask them what was happening, or to look.

"Swap," I said, crab-walking back to the bar and reaching up. "I got two bullets in each gun."

Horst did not have to be told twice. He could fire the Colts with his left hand, keep the machete in reserve. I could handle the shotgun.

"This is the last round for the shotgun," Horst said. "I'm out."

His voice was weak. He was losing blood, but there wasn't anything I could do about that right this moment.

I took the bowie knife.

"You ready up there?" I risked calling up the stairs.

"We are," Felicia called back, sounding quite cheerful. "And here they come!"

So far, Felicia and Isabella had been casting spells down the street, best I could tell. The enemy soldiers under the roof of the balcony were not in their sight. The doors would have been breached if the two witches hadn't been keeping the rest at bay.

I didn't know what damage Isabella's magic was causing. The noisier bangs were pure Felicia. She loved a good explosion.

I called, "Eli, can you help upstairs?"

"No," Eli said. "I'll try in a moment."

It really was him, he was really here, but something was awful wrong. I risked a glance, but it was so dark in the shadows of the barroom I couldn't tell what I was seeing.

That glance almost cost me my life. One of the bodies on the porch had more spunk in it than I had supposed. The soldier heaved himself up on his elbows and aimed at me through a hole in the door. If I hadn't fired the shotgun a fraction of a second faster than he fired his gun, it would have been all over for me. And that shotgun blast put paid to the doors, by the way. They were now more hole than wood.

I spared a second to think of my mother and to hope that she and Jackson were safe. Jackson wouldn't mind his hotel being ruined if my mother was unharmed.

There was a sort of electrical crackle over my head, followed by a loud pop and some screaming down the street. That must be Isabella. Interesting. Then a more familiar *boom* and yet more screaming. Felicia. I heard a big thud behind me and pivoted on my bootheels, still squatting. Horst had passed out.

Son of a bitch.

All right, then. I was by myself defending this entrance. I set the bowie knife by my feet. I checked behind the bar, hoping some shotgun shells had magically appeared—no—and took back my Colts from Horst, since he wouldn't be using them. I got into position in front of the bar to the left side of the doors.

I breathed in and out slowly. Time to gather myself.

This battle could not go on much longer. I didn't know why we were fighting or who was on the other side, but having started it, I was determined to win. There was a moving shadow at the remains of the doors.

I set my jaw, raised my right gun, and then I blew up.

For the second time in an hour, I landed on my back. My feet were toward the remains of the doors, my head at the foot of the staircase. I struggled to draw in air. Maybe I'd never be able. Maybe this was it.

Then the pressure released. I sucked in the beautiful smoky air, though it crackled in my chest. My scrabbling hand found the bowie knife. I gripped it in a way that meant business. A man whose smell was unfamiliar—blood, a dyed uniform, horse, unwashed skin—stood over me, and I stabbed upward with everything I had. He gave an awful groan and collapsed on top of me, and that was it. No light, no air. I left the fight.

But after that moment of blackness, I radiated light.

I could feel it surrounding me, I could feel voices outside its radiance, I could feel warmth creeping back into my cold limbs.

Without opening my eyes, I was the sun.

Until my light exploded.

CHAPTER TWENTY-FOUR

Felicia

It was crazy to think I'd heard Eli downstairs, but there was nothing I could do about it until I'd fought as hard as I could for as long as I could. Which was pretty hard and pretty long. Isabella and I killed the enemy to the best of our ability. A lull came, and I heard the guns roar downstairs and then a silence. I could actually hear myself breathing, and though the day had been hot, the night had a hint of chill.

"Who do you think they are?" I asked my aunt. It didn't feel right somehow to be killing people without having any idea why they were attacking you.

"The uniforms are the same as those of the soldiers you killed at the camp," she answered.

She calibrated the trajectory of her next crackly electrical ball before sending it out to arc over several yards to land in the midst of a clump of soldiers. She grinned. Seemed there were a few ways I was like my mother's family.

Isabella leaned over the edge of the balcony and looked down. "They're closer than we thought!" she said urgently. "Quick!"

We'd learned right away my bombs were faster than her electricity. I leaned over and placed an explosion directly under us. Even as it left my hand, I felt disaster in the air. The explosion would blow the air and broken wood inside, and anyone close to the remains of the doors would . . .

"Oh, my God," I said.

I went down the stairs pell-mell, cursing my aunt with all my might. Isabella had thought that through. She would not mind if I killed my sister, not at all. It would be even better than Isabella herself causing Lizbeth to die, to her thinking.

I got to the foot of the stairs and saw the most amazing sight. There was a dead man on top of my sister, and she was covered in blood. Her hand still gripped a knife in his side. Eli—*Eli*—was crawling toward her, and to help him . . . she was glowing with light.

I stopped in my tracks. Lizbeth glowed like the sun, which created a target for every soldier alive in the vicinity. The body weighing her down was lifting and floating off to her right. I had never seen anything so spooky, and considering I went to a school for spooky people, that was saying something.

I got over being paralyzed and leaped from the bottom stair to the remains of the doors to look outside. It was imperative I check the attention the light had drawn.

There was almost no movement to be seen, though the glow behind me was no help at all for my vision. So I stepped outside. There was a uniformed woman crawling for the shelter of the little porch of the dry goods store, but she collapsed and died as I noted her. A man farther down the street staggered to his feet and tried to get away, but I snatched the rest of his life from him and added it to my power by instinct. I had been depleted during the battle, and I needed strength.

I was sure Isabella could see me, but I was also sure she did not want to kill me, since she'd come here to add me to her . . . power base? Attraction? Stable? I took a few more steps into the darkness, my eyes adapting. I could hear gunfire off to the east but none to the west. Only a pop or two to the south in the direction of the hill.

I took a deep breath. I turned and went back inside.

I stepped over the pile of bodies in front of the doors and the smaller pile of those who had made it inside. Lizbeth was still glowing, but the power of the light was beginning to diminish. I knelt to her right. Eli had reached her left side.

"You came back," I said stupidly. "She thought you had left her for good. She thought you had gone back to your mother's."

"No," Eli said. "I would not leave her. I thought she would know that." He sounded incredulous.

And of all times to start arguing, this was the one I picked. "You prick! You told her how limited you felt in Segundo Mexia, how bored! You did not seem upset when she lost the baby!" I struggled to get more out, but I was defeated by the words I could not find.

Eli just shook his head. "I cried when she lost the baby. But where she could not see me. She had grief enough."

"And where is Peter?" I said, on the verge of weeping. "Why isn't he here?" Right by me, by my sister, by his brother.

"He is here," Eli said, and his voice was heavy as lead. He half-turned, pointed behind him into the shadow of one of the tables.

Beyond Eli, I saw the huddled form that had been Peter. He was dead.

And I felt like the ceiling fell on me.

CHAPTER TWENTY-FIVE

Lizbeth

When I woke up, it took me a minute to recall how I'd gotten where I was. Eli had carried me up the stairs. I'd been so happy to see him, but I couldn't speak.

The sun was coming in through the windows of the hotel room. I recognized the furnishings; it was the room over the porch, the one rented to Isabella. From the slant of the light, I guessed it was about two or three in the afternoon. The room was hot, though a fan was going in a corner. It was one of the new kind that rotated. I was surprised the electricity was working.

I wasn't sure what had happened to me.

I began by wiggling my fingers. Hands were okay. Wiggled my toes. Feet were okay. I touched my stomach and chest. No bullet holes but a vast, aching soreness. A couple of ribs were cracked. I could bend my knees and turn my head.

When I looked to my left, I could see Eli had fallen asleep in the chair by the bed, his head resting on the mattress on his folded arms. There were dried tearstains on his cheeks.

I looked to my right. My sister was asleep on the couch that came with the room. The door to the balcony was open, and I could hear noises coming from below. Hammering and sawing. Repair sounds.

I had to see if I could stand, because I had to get to the bathroom. I could see its doorway past Eli's head. I had to bite my lip while I maneuvered myself to sit up. Then I had to put my feet on the floor. Then I had to push myself off the bed and stand. Extremely painful but necessary.

I held on to the bedstead as I rounded the end and inched my way to that open bathroom door. The closer I got, the more I needed it. I was glad someone had taken my jeans off. I barely had time to slide my underwear down.

That was the best feeling I'd had in a long time.

When I was done, I shut the bathroom door so I could dull the sound of the flush. I turned to face the mirror, and boy, was I sorry. I was a wreck. I had blood spattered all over me, though someone had made an attempt to get it off my face, smearing it around in the process. I smelled, too: blood and magic and guns and death. I started the water running in the sink and washed my face and then my arms. I had to be very gentle patting drying myself with the towel.

I was black and blue.

The door opened a crack. Felicia peered in, saw I was moving, and came in with me, shutting the door behind her.

"You look worse than I do," I said slowly. I had to gasp for breath to talk, and that hurt.

"I hate to hear that. You look pretty damn bad." She tried to smile.

"My hair hurts."

She actually laughed.

"I washed my face," I pointed out.

"Maybe I will, too, after you stop hogging the mirror."

I can't say why we were bantering like this. I knew bad news was in her mouth to tell me. I didn't want to hear it. We were lucky to be alive. Apparently, we'd won the battle. Could we not settle for that for just a few minutes? An hour or two?

"So how come I'm so sore if I wasn't shot?" I asked at random.

"Isabella told me you were about to be attacked by someone coming through the front door, so I leaned over to blow this attacker up, and he wasn't there. You took the brunt of the explosion. Blew you backward."

"Where is Isabella?"

"I pushed her off the balcony. I was mad."

"Yeah, no kidding! Thank you! Ahm . . . do I remember shining?"

"I think that was all the magic I'd poured into you lately. It made it easy to find you when I got downstairs. Eli was beside you, too."

Felicia took a breath.

"He told me about Peter then."

"Told you what?" I closed my eyes, because we'd come to the bad thing.

"He got shot in the back when he and Eli were running into the hotel. He bled out."

I wobbled and would have landed on the floor if Felicia hadn't caught me. She eased me down on the toilet lid.

I didn't have the strength to bawl, but tears began to stream down my cheeks.

"You couldn't bring him back?"

She shook her head. "I'd used up all my juice. I had nothing left." She hesitated. "Even if I'd been all charged up, he'd lost so much blood, and he'd been dead for over thirty minutes . . . I don't know if he'd have been the same Peter."

"Does his mom know?" I whispered.

"Eli will tell her when the telegraph lines are repaired."

"What the hell did they want? Why was Segundo Mexia the target? Who in their right mind would want this town?"

The bathroom door opened again. This time, it was Eli.

"I heard you talking, so I figured you were awake and not, um, using the facilities."

"I'm so sorry," I said. "I'm so sorry." Those were the only words I could think of to say.

"I can't believe I've lost my brother, the only one worth a damn. And I almost lost you, too."

"You came back. Why did you come back? I thought you were gone for good."

Felicia slipped out of the bathroom. It was a strange place to have this conversation, but that was where we were, and we were having it.

"I thought I might be. I got a telegram from a Brazilian magician named Chin-Hao Costa. I met him at a conference two years ago. He said I was needed urgently in San Diego, if I could risk coming there. Two days, he said, was all he needed, but it was life or death. And he said there was a lot of money involved. I wanted our life to be better."

"I'll bet you got there and couldn't find him."

"How did you know?"

"He got you away so he could come here instead. He rescued Felicia from a kidnapper, long story short, and got her trust. I wonder if that was a setup all along. Felicia thinks he was the one who killed me."

"He killed you?" Eli looked horrified, and helpless. "What do you mean? How are you here?"

"I feel like I've died a lot while you were gone," I said. And if I sounded bleak and also angry, I don't think you could blame me. "I expect Chin-Hao wanted you out of the way so he could court

Felicia. And I was more of a rock in the way than he expected. He killed me in my sleep. Felicia found me in time and brought me back."

"I'll kill him," Eli said, very calmly.

"If Felicia did her work right, he's already dead."

"Good girl," Eli said. "No wonder Peter likes . . . " And then he remembered, and his smile was snuffed out.

I asked him about his trip to San Diego, just to get his mind away from Peter for a moment. "Did you see your mother? She's well?"

"Yes," he said, hesitantly. "I thought I'd be so glad to be in the house with my family. But my family wasn't there."

I'm such an idiot. I opened my mouth to ask him where they were.

"And before you ask," he said neatly, "you are my family."

I closed my mouth again.

"My mother had gotten a telegram from you."

"Mom made me send it. She said your mother would know where you were, and she'd get you to respond."

"Well, sort of right. She told me she'd gotten one. I had to find it in her wastebasket to see what you had said. What family information did I need to know?"

"My mother's having a baby. Her and Jackson," I added, ridiculously.

"Well. That's really big news." Eli took a deep breath. "I can't tell you how sorry I am that I was a jerk about the baby. I was trying to act strong for you, but I left you thinking I didn't care."

"I thought you were okay with me losing the baby. I thought you didn't want to have a child with me."

"Who else would I have a baby with?" he said, actually seeming confused. "You're my wife."

"You didn't seem to feel that way when I miscarried." That was as blunt as blunt could be.

"I cared very much. I just didn't know what to do about it, and I couldn't make you feel better, so I acted like a tough guy. That's what I do when I don't know what else I can do. That's how I was raised."

I looked hard at him. That sounded so dumb. Could Eli be that misguided?

I decided he could.

"Will you ever do that again?" I wanted to be sure.

"I might. It's what my father always did."

"You see how that worked out for him," I said.

Eli nodded. "I have cried my tears over Peter," he said softly.

"Peter was a very good brother, and he loved you."

Eli was crying again now. When he could talk, he said, "It only took a minute. He didn't even know what had happened. That's all he said. 'What hit me?' I knew he was dead and that you needed help, but for a few minutes, I . . . couldn't move."

"Where is Peter's body?" I said.

"I took him to Fedderman's. They are very busy, of course. But Peter has top priority."

That was the only funeral home in town, so I'd figured that was where Peter was.

I heard someone on the stairs. There was a knock at the door to our room. Time to leave the bathroom. Eli helped me stand and walk, and when I was back on the bed, he said, "Come in."

I was glad to see Mom and Jackson, with my sister trailing behind them. Mom knew about Peter, which was a relief, and she and Jackson gave Eli their condolences.

Mom asked the questions I'd been longing to ask. She made it seem natural to want to know where Peter would be buried, if Eli's family had a plot in San Diego, or if the Segundo Mexia cemetery would be a possibility.

It was hard to believe they were talking about Peter. I had watched Peter turn from an impulsive kid into a likable and responsible young man. I had seen him love my sister. He had always been kind to me, he had always enjoyed every moment he had of life after his father had died, and he would have had many happy years, I was sure. Now Peter would be dust.

I tried to imagine Peter with Eli's unborn baby. He would have been a good uncle. And that made me start crying.

Felicia came to sit on the side of the bed. She hadn't made up her mind about their relationship. Now she'd never have to. I could see that was making her more miserable, rather than less.

I could not even begin to measure the grief Eli was suffering. He and Peter had stood together against their father and their older brothers. They had balanced each other. Now Eli did not know what to do without his brother in the same world.

All the construction noise downstairs was scratching at my nerves.

When silence fell for a moment, I said, "Eli, can we go home?"

My mother protested that I didn't look like I could walk that far, but Jackson read me correctly.

"She needs to be in her own place, Candle," he said, and Mom clamped her lips shut.

I wanted to go home so badly I could scream.

I felt so up and down. I was alive. Eli had returned, and he would stay with me! But Peter was dead. And Felicia had killed her aunt for tricking my sister into killing me. Wait. She'd said she'd pushed Isabella off the balcony. Did that mean Isabella was for sure dead?

I don't know how we three made it up the hill to the cabin. Eli helped, carrying me part of the way. Felicia gave me shoves of magic when I walked. When we reached it, we had no visitors of any sort, and it was quiet. Chrissie's children hushed the minute they saw us. Maybe our appearance was enough to scare them silent. We were all stained bloody.

I made my way to our bed and lay down and waited for my muscles to quit screaming at me.

A little later, Chrissie brought over two largemouth bass her husband had caught, which was very handsome of her. I had been forgiven for frightening her. Chrissie came into the bedroom to talk to me for a minute, and she told me the names of the townspeople who had been killed the night before. Horst was one of them. They hadn't been able to stop the bleeding in his shoulder, and he had gone into convulsions and quit breathing.

I hadn't even asked Jackson how Horst was doing. I felt ashamed.

Annie Lee Wilkins, a classmate of mine who made extra money by sewing, had gotten hit by a stray bullet. John Seahorse had been hit in the head by one of the soldiers, shattering his skull. Emmie inherited, Chrissie said with some surprise.

She kept on going. A ne'er-do-well named Taylor Benitez had been found dead in an alley, but that might have been a case of someone who'd been mad at Taylor taking the opportunity to settle a score. I waited, but Chrissie didn't mention any guest of the Antelope being among the dead. Felicia hadn't found Isabella's body.

The pile of dead soldiers was testament to how tough citizens of Segundo Mexia could be.

But all that death begged the question.

Why had we been attacked?

I heard the craziest rumors in the days following.

The dead men and women were all from New America, and they had been attempting to annex land to the south of their border.

The dead men and women had all been from the Holy Russian

Empire, and they had been charged with bringing Eli back to trial for some unspecified crime.

The dead men and women had all belonged to a sort of consortium of bandits, and they had wanted to seize our town for their hideout.

The night before he left to accompany Peter's coffin back to San Diego, Eli told me what he knew.

The small army had been recruited from people who'd been evicted from other military groups. Some from the New America militia, a peacekeeping force that was only sometimes on the side of law and order; some from the people who could not abide the discipline of being in any one of the Holy Russian Empire military groups (border police, royal bodyguards, police department, and so on); and some from convicted gunslingers who wanted out of jail enough to "volunteer."

They'd targeted Segundo Mexia because it seemed like a good location for their permanent base. Not too far south of New America, not too far north of Mexico, and a good distance away from the HRE, which had a notoriously long arm. Using our isolated town as their center of operations, the American Security Force had planned to gradually increase their holdings, absorbing the nearby towns until they were a force to be reckoned with. A private army.

"But who led them? Who funded them? This wasn't a cheap operation."

We were in our bed together, and though I was too tender and pained for any demonstration of love, talking privately one-to-one was just as good. I'd had a good long look at a future without the companionship of Eli. That future had been bleak.

"I can't be sure," Eli warned me. "But two people who were investigating told me they felt Iron Hand had a stake in it."

I could not imagine a private investigating and security firm planning to take over part of the country. I said as much.

"It does seem like a huge waste of money," Eli said, turning on his side to face me. "But just imagine that you worked for Iron Hand. They would have loved to have you, you know that. Then just imagine that the best gunnies and most reckless grigoris joined them, too, with enough cannon fodder to enforce the rules."

"They'd be running things in no time," I said, after I'd thought about it. "Not me, 'cause I don't want to. But lots of people who feel left out would want to join up. They'd get some power and some say-so."

"Eventually, Iron Hand would make enough money to offset the expenses," Eli said. "The only country with enough army to face them down is the HRE or Canada."

I started to argue, but then I realized he was right. "Dixie's too poor to have a great army. I don't think they'd be keen to fight unless they were protecting their home ground," I said. "New England? They wouldn't care unless it was right at their border. And this army wouldn't go up as far as Canada or as far south as the denser part of Mexico."

"Easy pickings here," said Eli. "It's a poor part of the former United States, but there are minerals here that are probably worth a lot. Silver and copper, for example."

"Huh," I said.

We lay together in silence. I could hear a faint snore from Felicia's room. She would be going back to San Diego with Eli, to complete her schooling and become an accredited grigori. The Wizards' Ball would be in seven months. That would determine her future unless she had another idea, which was entirely possible.

I felt sleep pulling me down, but I had one more thing to say to my husband.

"Eli, if you ever do decide to leave me, tell me to my face."

"You have my word. Why?"

"It made me crazy, not knowing. I had no reply for people wondering where you were. And my heart hurt."

"You're getting very flowery in your maturity, Lizbeth!"

"Imagine being in my place," I suggested. "Having no idea where you were, why you'd left, if you intended to return."

"I'd go crazy," he said. "You know I would. I really didn't think my good-bye was open to a different interpretation. But I know now that I was not clear at all."

"This isn't what you foresaw when you looked at your future." I waved my hand, indicating the wooden walls and the plain furnishings, me, Segundo Mexia.

"No, it isn't," he said honestly. "But I did know my traitorous father might sink my boat, so to speak, and he did. Also, I didn't know I would get lucky and meet an incredible woman."

Who wouldn't feel warm and cozy after hearing that?

"I'm glad to hear you say so," I admitted. "I know you feel your ability isn't being used to its highest level, here and now. But there is time for that to happen. In the meantime, the magic you work is really helping people here. That has to feel at least a little bit good?"

"It feels a lot good," he assured me. "And we'll stand by your sister during the ball, make sure she finds the right person."

I was pretty sure Felicia could handle that herself, but I wasn't going to turn down a chance to be on hand.

Jackson had brought me the newspapers that day, and I had read them page by page.

"Have you heard about this crazy man in Germany?" I asked, my voice already slow and drowsy.

"We'll talk about him another time," Eli murmured. "His name is Hitler."

ABOUT THE AUTHOR

Charlaine Harris is a *New York Times* and *USA Today* bestselling author who has been in print for more than thirty years. She has written four series and two stand-alone novels, in addition to numerous short stories, novellas, and graphic novels (cowritten with Christopher Golden). Her Sookie Stackhouse novels have appeared in twenty-five different languages and on worldwide bestseller lists. They're also the basis of the acclaimed HBO series *True Blood*. Harris has co-edited five anthologies with Leigh Perry (Toni L.P. Kelner). Harris now lives on a cliff overlooking the Brazos River. When she's not writing, she's an omnivorous reader, and she's also surrounded by rescue dogs.